MW01138529

LITTLE MRS. COLLINS

Charlotte Lucas; A young lady without Pride or Prejudice

PEGGY TULIP

ISBN: 978-1-4834-8178-4 (sc)
ISBN: 978-1-4834-8177-7 (e)

Lulu Publishing Services rev. date: 02/05/2019

For

Jo Liz Marit Gillian Hilda Marion Angela and
Barbara who gave me an Imprimatur.

That the Longbourn estate was entailed to Mr. Bennet's next male heir was known to all who had been within hearing distance of Mr. Bennet's indignant wife. Rumour that the Arch Rascal had imposed himself upon their home at Longbourn caused a general raising of eyebrows in the neighbourhood and would have sparked much indignation and speculation had the neighbours not already been in the grip of a high fever preparing for the grandest social event of the year, Mr. Bingley's Ball at Netherfield Park.

Charlotte Lucas was in the first dance of the Ball before she saw her friend Elizabeth Bennet, also in the dance, and partly concealed by a tall dark haired stranger who was obviously a stranger to dancing. Oh Dear! That would not please Lizzie! Charlotte's amusement at her friend's predicament faded as the stranger, turning with the dance, revealed to her a face that so engaged and quickened her interest that it took her breath away. She was watching transfixed as the pleasing face turned and then bestowed a captivated look upon Lizzie's face as he took her hand again in the dance and turned away. She was suddenly numb, paralyzed.

"Miss Lucas?" She had missed her step.

She forced herself back to the dance, completed it somehow, then fled to a chair by the wall. She was not herself. Good sense and wildest emotion strove within her absorbing all physical strength. She was fighting back tears that threatened to engulf and disgrace her when Elizabeth, who had been searching for her, noticed nothing amiss as she flung herself, angry and indignant, onto a chair alongside.

"Mr. Darcy has forbidden Mr. Bingley to invite Mr. Wickham to the ball." The threatening tears mercifully receded as Charlotte summoned her scattered wits to untangle this sentence. Mr. Wickham, a recent recruit to the militia stationed near Meryton, had caused a stir among the young ladies. Charlotte, strangely immune to uniforms, had not yet met him.

"You must not slander Mr. Bingley so. You know that can't be true."

"Mr. Wickham isn't here."

"And when you see him you can ask him why."

"I spoke to his particular friend. He says Mr. Darcy's presence kept him away."

Mr. Darcy, a stately young gentleman from Derbyshire was currently on a visit to Netherfield Park. He had recently accompanied his friend Mr. Bingley to a ball at the Meryton Assembly Rooms, where he had seemed over haughty and had slighted Lizzie by declining an opportunity to dance with her. The general opinion was much against him.

"Lizzie Bennet! If the presence of Mr. Bingley's house guest at a ball in Mr. Bingley's house was going to spoil your evening, you should never have accepted his invitation."

"Oh Charlotte! You're right of course."

"Lizzie, you have revealed your particular partiality for Mr. Wickham and your great displeasure at Mr. Darcy. Be careful how freely you speak."

"I'm speaking to you, Charlotte. We can tell each other anything."

Alas! This was no longer true. Charlotte could not even explain to herself the sudden perverse waves of intense emotion that had overwhelmed her. Suddenly, the cause of it was standing before them. Charlotte, daring to look at him, took up her fan to hide her cheeks as her blood quickened. That he might be the un-met, raised within her mixed feelings of joy and dread that once more rendered her helpless. When introductions were completed he turned to Elizabeth.

"Cousin, here is a wonderful coincidence. Mr. Darcy of Pemberley is present. He is the nephew of my benefactress. Pray introduce me, I must make myself known." Mr. Collins was almost dancing with delight.

Elizabeth looked at him in horror and then at Mr. Darcy where he stood, serious faced, nearby in conversation with Mr. Bingley and his sisters. She was silent, paralyzed by reluctance. The last thing she wanted was to draw the attention of Mr. Darcy.

"Don't worry cousin. Formality gives way before family connection." He turned to Charlotte. "He is the gentleman with our host?" Charlotte, melting before his dark blue eyes could only nod. He excused himself and left them to approach Mr. Darcy.

"Oh!" Elizabeth exhaled a blast of exasperation. "How embarrassing! And we must tolerate him until Saturday!" She rushed away displeased with the incident, with herself, and with her new relation.

Charlotte, further confused by Lizzie's oddness was in turmoil. The spark ignited within her would not be denied. She had responded to the un-met instinctively and been stung by the way he had looked at Lizzie. She longed to be at home. She was in jeopardy of making an exhibition of herself but there were dances on her card that she must honour.

She moved in a daze towards the shelter of her mother and the older ladies and emerged from their midst only for those to whom she was already engaged, lest the un-met should seek to engage her. She feared that if he did, she might not be able to answer and was certain that she would not be able to stand. The strain exhausted her. Lady Lucas detected low spirits as they were driven home and her father reminded her that tomorrow they were to begin a two day visit to London, surely that would revive her spirits. Charlotte agreed, solely as a means of putting an end to the conversation.

She remained in her room next morning and watched from the window as the carriage took her parents to London. Their surprise at her request to be excused the excursion delayed their departure by quite thirty minutes with anxious discussion as to whether they should summon the physician or whether Lady Lucas should remain at home. She had convinced them that she felt in no way unwell but may have over exerted herself in the excitements of the previous evening. This was not really an untruth, and when she insisted that she would not enjoy the pleasures that they were anticipating, they were assured that she had better remain at home.

She had diagnosed her malady during the drive home from Netherfield and in the privacy of her room had dared to name it. Lovesickness. The invention, she had always thought, of poets and romancers but now she felt the pain and the power of its reality. So long as the object of that pain and power was at Longbourn, it must draw her like a magnet. It did not make her happy, it made her miserable, but she was powerless before it. She must take what she could from it until Saturday, after that the old life would resume, leaving her with a precious deep wound that might heal in a lifetime. Or, she feared, she may have discovered at last that she had a heart only to have it broken by her dearest friend Lizzie Bennet.

She took comfort from the fact that her friend had no interest at all in Mr. Collins. Elizabeth was clearly infatuated with a man called Wickham.

Charlotte Lucas was unobtrusive by nature but she was not passive. From infancy she displayed a firm chin, a pair of calm grey eyes and an amiable acceptance of the world. Natural curiosity, pre-occupied parents and a solitary childhood had made her a keen and careful observer. She drew conclusions from what she observed but did not attract attention by voicing them.

Her father had a warehouse in London and a smaller store in Merryton dealing in spices, nuts, dried fruits and various exotic comestibles. The expanding business had over-flowed into their home and absorbed the interest of both parents, and although she was constantly in their presence she did not receive more of their attention than was necessary.

She had sensed a change of atmosphere in the life of the family as she passed her tenth birthday. As she outgrew her clothes they were replaced, garment for garment, boot for boot, but in a higher quality. The store in Meryton was closed. There were more frequent visits to London by her father, and now her mother went with him. The Lucases had always kept an excellent table, her father was, after all, a warehouseman, but the quality of the linen, china and plate that replaced that of her youth enhanced the pleasure of dining and was a compliment to guests who seemed to come in increasing numbers. All this she observed, approved, and enjoyed.

She had a moment of alarm when her father announced his intention of buying her a piano. She implored him not to consider it because she had noticed that those with proficiency were called upon to draw attention to themselves, and she would dislike that above all things. What she longed for, she told him, was someone to satisfy her curiosity, answer her questions. A succession of tutors for two hours, two days each week, provided a skeleton of intellectual satisfaction over the years and she came to value deeper learning in others.

When she was twelve years old the change acquired a momentum that left the family breathless. By her thirteenth birthday her father was a Knight Bachelor and a City Liveryman, her mother was Lady Lucas and they were about to remove into a splendid new home being built for them in the nearby countryside. Leaving her home in Meryton caused Charlotte real heartache, she truly loved the old house in which she had been born and where she had spent her life. She had been relieved beyond expressing to hear her mother state a clear wish that under no circumstances was the house to be sold, since although she may not live there, she would not part with it.

There had been few excitements in her young life. Chief among them was the before-Christmas visit to her father's London warehouse. She always thrillingly anticipated the deep spicy smells that made her cough and the ritual tasting of scented sweet-meats, raisins, dates, new kinds of nuts and strange fruits crispy with sugar, especially those dangerous little pieces of ginger that started with deceptive sweetness then exploded into her mouth.

One year, when she had wandered away from the moving legs and the men's conversations, she found herself in the presence of a black cat on a sack in a dark corner. It was nuzzling a tiny black kitten and as she watched, fascinated, it magically produced another, and set about licking it mercilessly, glancing all the while at Charlotte who was mesmerized and rooted to the spot. Hearing her father's laugh she had run towards it, back to the babble of noise, and found her father and clutched at him with relief but shared nothing of the mystery she had witnessed.

Since it was the general view that Charlotte, the only child of Sir William and Lady Lucas, was a commodity of high value in the marriage market, it was natural that Charlotte herself should share that view. She was content to think that somewhere, as yet un-met, there was a young man who would gain the approval of herself and her parents, and that her life in the world as an adult with her own establishment could begin.

Fate, however, had not yet done with changes to the Lucas family. Weeks after the removal to Lucas Lodge, Charlotte was informed by a pink-cheeked mother, that she should prepare herself for a younger sibling. Her own powers of observation had already warned her but she smiled on her mother and truthfully expressed delight. She was at a loss when, visiting her friend Jane Bennet for tutoring by Jane's father on the rivers of England, she was greeted at the door of Longbourn with, "Oh Charlotte! We were very sorry to hear about your mother." Jane, at ten years old was almost as tall as Charlotte and had a deceptively mature air. Her concern seemed genuine. Elizabeth, much smaller, was dancing with excitement, wide round eyes fixed on Charlotte's face. She looked at them not comprehending.

"We heard our mother tell Aunt Philips that it cannot be safe after so many years." Said Elizabeth, breathlessly. Mr. Bennet, overhearing the conversation through the part open door of his library, half rose to intervene then settled again acknowledging himself powerless. Jane was distressed and Elizabeth remorseful as they looked at Charlotte's stricken face. Charlotte was seized by an emotion of outrage so new to her and so intense that it made her gasp. She pressed a firm hand on the shoulder of each girl.

"Do you not know how shocking it is for me to hear that? And how much more shocking it would be for my mother to hear it?" She raised her voice, addressing the house at large. "*Nobody* is to say it again, ever. Do you understand? *Nobody.*" The girls nodded solemnly. "Besides," she continued in a voice sharpened by anger, "It just isn't true. I will have a sister or brother and anyone who has said otherwise will be shown to be a .....*ninny*. Who would you put your faith in Mother Bennet or Mother Nature?"

Mr. Bennet relaxed, and before his daughters could consider an answer to the question, called out.

"Young ladies, if Charlotte has come let us make a start on the river Thames. Anyone who cannot spell the word need come no further than the door."

Mother Nature delivered to Lady Lucas all she had promised in the form of a healthy baby girl. She repeated the process two years later and after a further two years astounded all expectations with a robust baby boy. Babies reigned in the Lucas household. Each succeeding child devalued Charlotte on the marriage market and she became gradually incorporated as an honorary parent. She loved her younger siblings without reservation and they taught her as much as she ever taught them.

Her pleasure at the weddings of younger relations and friends never diminished, though her canny assessment of how each marriage might fare became more acute and she had, with increasing frequency, been present at the christening of one or other of the happy pair. As her own birthdays accumulated up to and beyond twenty, she felt an occasional nostalgia for her younger self, awaiting the un-met one who would engage her interest and share her establishment, but she was always much too usefully and happily occupied with practical or intellectual matters to indulge it and it quickly passed. Her heart had never been touched. In her twentieth year she had firmly packed away a sizeable collection of goods, bought with pleasure in her teenage years for her own future establishment. Reviewing them had become a decreasing pleasure. However, since such things would always be useful, their existence did not make her sad and she was by way of forgetting just what they were.

Small town social life in Meryton followed its seasonal round with easy intercourse between acquaintances and the added interest of occasional visiting strangers. At least two balls a year at the Assembly Rooms gave the young ladies the opportunity to be seriously anxious about what they would wear, and other more informal gatherings served to keep their feet nimble. Friendships warmed and cooled but Charlotte's firmest friendship was with Elizabeth Bennet. The shocking exchange between the girls, years ago, had bound Elizabeth to Charlotte with a high regard and Charlotte had responded to the spontaneous, and frequently unguarded, truthfulness of the growing girl. Near neighbours, the girls met frequently. Mrs. Bennet bearing the long grudge of 'Mother Bennet or Mother Nature' was unable to prevent the friendship but could never say anything remotely complimentary about Charlotte Lucas. Her husband, on the other hand, accorded her a guarded respect.

CHAPTER

3

Late in the morning Charlotte set her feet towards Longbourn, uncertain whether Mr. Collins would be present and whether, if he were, it would be would be pleasing or unendurable to be in his company. She found herself his sole companion. He had proposed marriage to Elizabeth and been refused. The family, except for Mrs. Bennet, was avoiding him and he was avoiding Mrs. Bennet.

Charlotte never expected calm at Longbourn but the confusion that greeted her that morning shocked her. Lizzie's younger sisters, Kitty and Lydia, competed in hysteria and volume to give a version of the event and her own confusions multiplied then evaporated before it.

She saw the imploring desperate look with which he recognized her as his long legs sped down the staircase to the hall, and could not escape the hand with which, astonishingly, he grasped the edge of her sleeve and pulled her by the wrist back out of the front door, fleeing Mrs. Bennet's voice. He found them a refuge on a seat in the shrubbery before he released the wrist, apparently unaware that he had taken it. She rested it on her knee feeling the strong residual grip, a straw clutched by a drowning man. One of her first tutors, thrilling her with stories of Classical myth, had acquainted her with Cupid, the wilful careless boy. She had never imagined such cruelty until now.

Mr. Collins, overwhelmed, head down, stiff and eaten up by what had occurred, was silent. Because it would be the last time she would ever see him she looked at him carefully, liking what she saw and grieving its loss. As he constantly attempted to retrieve some dignity and then let it slip away again, he put her in mind of a younger sibling, chastised and uncertain, angry and helpless. She broke the silence.

"Take some deep breaths Mr. Collins."

"I have been most shamefully scorned!" The furious angry explosion startled Charlotte. Watching him, she took some time to consider it then she expressed her conclusion.

"Your pride has been humbled, Sir. But your heart is not broken."

That his heart was unbroken seemed immaterial to him. It was everything to Charlotte. He raised his head and looked at her, his eyes, deep blue and sparked by anger. His mouth was bitter and his statement was bitter.

"I was misled."

She feared that this may be true but it was not a topic to be dwelt upon.

"Come, Mr. Collins, you are an educated man. You know that for every contract there must be an offer and an acceptance. My father is a merchant. When he makes an offer for goods he does not humiliate himself, the man who refuses that offer does not scorn it. Marriage is a contract. You did not humiliate yourself by making the offer. Elizabeth in refusing it did not scorn it."

She was easier now. For sure, a heart-broken man would be grieving alone or packing in haste to quit Longbourn and return home.

"If you were misled, or even if you think you were misled, you cannot believe that it was done with malice."

She marvelled at the pleasure she felt simply to sit in his presence, but wondered if he was aware of the risk he had taken, the consequences of today's proposal could have been far reaching. She was heartened that he listened to what she said. In the course of it, the bitter, angry look had left his face, and the face was pleasing.

"I am a great admirer of Elizabeth. She is my closest friend. I know that she would not scorn you, but you should be grateful to her for her good sense in refusing you, unless it was your generous intention to house and provide for his whole family after Mr. Bennet's death."

He started in his seat.

"Oh Miss Lucas!" He dropped back, covering his face. She observed the handsome hands, the tapering fingers.

Charlotte, long a tutor to her younger siblings, recognized a lesson gone home and changed the subject.

"Is your church a pre-Reformation church Mr. Collins?"

It was not. The change of topic gave him opportunity to recover his presence of mind rapidly and with relief. He spoke proudly and lovingly of his church of St. Andrew at Hunstan, which was built some little time after the building of Wren's cathedral in London which was so large and grand. St. Andrew's had no pretension to grandeur, it was plain and lowly but well windowed with good joinery, gated pews and the luxury of a musicians' gallery. Then he spoke in admiration of the patroness who had bestowed this Benefice upon him, and of her home, Rosings, and the elegance of her park. Then, more to the point, he described the smaller perfections of his own modest Parsonage, garden and glebe. Charlotte formed in her mind an establishment to cherish. He had been there but six months and any errors of taste made in only six months could be easily remedied. The mere sound of his voice and the fluency with which he spoke of architecture, history and horticulture held her entranced; simply to sit near him and look on him filled her with happiness.

She described life in Meryton, indicated the direction and closeness of her home, Lucas Lodge; enlarged upon her parents, currently on a visit to London, a city with which she, herself, was becoming increasingly familiar. She had, indeed, worshipped at that very St. Paul's, which she agreed was magnificent beyond description. She mentioned her younger siblings, carefully giving their respective ages including clearly, in passing, her own.

Despite the coolness of the day they had spoken for almost a full hour and when she rose to pay her respects to Mrs. Bennet, she felt

PEGGY TULIP

his reluctance at her departure. He followed her to the house, which was quiet. Charlotte guessed that the girls had escaped to Meryton. He went with her to Mrs. Bennet's little sitting room but remained beyond the open door. Mrs. Bennet was asleep from exhaustion and her daughter Mary, looking up from a book, would have disturbed her but for Charlotte's shake of the head. Charlotte barely hesitated before she took it upon herself to tell Mary to let Mrs. Bennet know that the family, including their guest if still with them, was invited to dine on the day following the next, at Lucas Lodge.

She returned home in an altered frame of mind. She had learned much about his circumstances and had revealed much of her own. Mr. Collins had a day in which to collect himself and return to his Parsonage but she hoped that he would come and meet her parents. She resigned herself to not seeing him on the morrow or, heart-stopping thought, perhaps never again.

She had intervened in her own fate for the first time since she persuaded her father not to buy a piano. It ought to make her uneasy but it made her strangely excited.

The Lucases and the Bennets dined regularly together and the presence of the younger members of both families usually ensured a lively party. For Charlotte the day had an added piquancy the moment she saw Mr. Collins but she sensed, at once, that she had subjected him to an ordeal. He appeared uneasy and awkward in the company of the Bennets. He gave her an earnest look but without smiling. Clearly, he was carrying his recent embarrassments with him and the giggling whisperings of Lydia and Kitty Bennet, whatever their cause, unnerved him. Lizzie had very sensibly excused herself on the pretext of a sore throat, and Jane was being as solicitous to him, as one could be to a broken heart. As they gathered before dinner he could not be still and when young Lucas, not very hopefully wondered if anyone would like to see his rabbits, he leaped to his feet and followed, unbalancing a small table as he went. They had to be summoned to dinner and their boots made clean.

At dinner Mary Bennet, encouraged by her mother, was eager to know which were his favourite psalms while volunteering quotations from her own. Sir William and Lady Lucas, sophisticated hosts, gave him every opportunity to offer experiences from his own life but he hardly responded, saying only that Rosings was the most beautiful house he had ever seen, and quickly inserting 'apart from the Parsonage'. He looked at her hopelessly as he said it. She wondered why he had not escaped and gone there, and had the intoxicating thought that he had stayed to see her. Her response was a bright, conspiratorial smile. She saw a quick lightening of his features, before the attention of all was drawn back to the psalms by Mary Bennet and to Mr. Bennet instructing her to keep them for a Sunday.

Charlotte would not allow Hope to possess her until their parting when he managed, with much contriving, to ask discreetly for a meeting next morning before he left Hertfordshire.

Mrs. Bennet, before departing, had managed to acquaint Lady Lucas with the shocking events of the previous Wednesday and Lady Lucas was relating them to her husband when Charlotte rejoined them.

"Why did you not tell us Charlotte? Why did you invite him to dine?"

Explanation was impossible.

"Mr. Collins has asked me for a meeting tomorrow morning," she gave Hope her head. "I anticipate that when he leaves, he and I may have an Understanding."

She left them, much startled, to make sense of it if they could, and withdrew to her own room. What she had to determine, in the event of an Understanding, was how much time must decently elapse between one proposal and the next. Eager and anxious as she was, she knew that it could not be less than six months. She resigned herself, reminding herself, and Hope, that this was still a daydream. She anticipated a sleepless night but slept soundly.

Sir William and Lady Lucas were stunned. They had long ceased to anticipate the invaluable Charlotte's departure from the family as a bride, and had half planned a future for her that kept her close. Lady Lucas was particularly restless, her unexpressed view that their visitor was too juvenile and gauche for the garb he wore, and seemed not to be entirely in control of his elbows and knees, manifested itself in strange dreams from which she was glad to escape even though it was not yet daylight.

When the morning was advanced Charlotte walked out to meet Mr. Collins. She was nervous, and determined not to be the first one to speak. She saw him over a low hedge as he approached; his gait was slow, his face troubled. He looked like a man who had come to take his leave, carrying on his shoulder a small leather satchel of personal belongings. He did not notice her. Head down, he was totally self-absorbed.

"Good morning, Mr.Collins!" She was smiling, cheerful. He stopped, then hurried towards her, but with no responding smile.

"Miss Lucas, when I leave Hertfordshire I am not likely to see you again."

"You will not return to Longbourn?"

"I think it very unlikely." He pulled a wry face. Charlotte, beset by disappointed hopes, could not speak. "Miss Lucas will you have me?"

"As a visitor?" Her heart leaped. "I am sure my parents will agree to that."

"As a husband."

"Yes.

"Are you sure?" He seemed surprised.

"Are *you* sure?"

"Yes!"

"Then I am sure." Charlotte heard her own hysterical laugh. "This is a very curious conversation we are having Mr. Collins."

William and Elizabeth Lucas had a special deep affection for Charlotte, their only child for several years and, since then, a trustworthy guide and guardian for the younger family. As her prospects for marriage diminished while her hours of tutoring accumulated, they had decided that she would have her childhood home to live in and develop as a school. They had considered her thirtieth birthday, three years hence, a suitable time to make the gift. Yesterday's mention of an 'understanding' had made Sir William waver, but Lady Lucas had no doubt that it should convert into a dowry and was persuasive.

Mr. Collins, eager to assure his prospective father-in-law that he was a man capable of raising and supporting a family, extracted from his satchel, documents prepared previously for his cousin Bennet. Sir William, quite at ease, invited his wife to see if there might not be a bottle of Madeira? The ladies left, and the gentlemen sat down to talk. After a decent interval a servant brought the wine and after a further interval mother and daughter re-entered, to find prospective bride-groom and father-in-law in harmonious accord. Consent having been given, the proposal was made and accepted with the blessing of the parents, and Charlotte was very surprised to learn that the house in Meryton was to be her dowry. The gentlemen had a second glass of Madeira and the ladies joined them; Lady Lucas then led her husband away and left the newly betrothed couple.

Charlotte was very deeply moved by the gift of her childhood home. Instinctively she detected her mother's hand behind it and deduced the earlier, deeper, motive. She turned her attention back to Mr. Collins. Happiness gave way to unease. He had withdrawn his attention and sat with gaze averted, face troubled. Her resolution faltered. She took his empty glass and placed it with her own on the table, then stood before him. She spoke softly, sad but practical.

"It is not too late Mr. Collins. We are not married yet. All that has been done can be undone in a moment."

He leaped to his feet and grasped her hands, holding them at chest height; the first time he had touched her since his arrival.

"Oh don't say that Miss Lucas! We must be married! We shall be married! But I have….."

His spontaneous gesture and double declaration took her completely by surprise. Her love was grateful and boundless whatever he had done. She squeezed the hands in her own and felt a responding pressure. She invited him to sit and they did so, holding hands. He made two attempts, and at the third, revealed that he had not told his cousin of his visit to Lucas Lodge. He had intended only to declare himself, but on seeing her, could not wait to know if she would have him, and since he had the necessary documents with him he had acted without … He stopped in mid-sentence and sighed hopelessly. His cousin, Mr. Bennet, had no expectation of their betrothal. He raised his head to look her in the eyes, and found them filling with tears. Concern brought him to his knees before her, and she bent her forehead lightly to touch his own and thus they remained for a few moments before she urged him back to his seat.

"Did his cousin need to be told? Did he need to know? Did anybody need to know - apart from Lady Catherine?" Mr. Collins, distracted, was wondering aloud.

Charlotte looked on him lovingly. It was too late for the Understanding and the decent lapse of six months. She expressed her view that the long friendship between the two families made a deceit of that magnitude impossible. He could see that was the case and would go now and tell Mr. Bennet. As he made to rise she retained his hands in hers. She thought it would be very sad if his recent reconciliation with Mr. Bennet was put in jeopardy by an incautious word spoken by either of them during an interview, which must by its very nature, generate considerable heat. He saw the good sense in that. She confessed she would like to break the news to Elizabeth herself, would he agree to that? He would, and nodded eagerly. Perhaps her father was the best person to break the news to his friend Mr. Bennet? He nodded again. Charlotte had watched a long flickering variety of panicked expressions from the blue eyes, before they settled and locked on her own steady gaze. The last one she decided must be relief. It made her smile and she got a smile in return.

He left Lucas Lodge, a happy man trying to conceal his happiness, to bid his cousins farewell and take the coach. Charlotte went to her room. She was still and quiet, re-visiting in her mind the events of the past four days, willing herself to believe them.

CHAPTER 6

The problem of how to approach Elizabeth resolved itself when Charlotte glimpsed her from the window as she entered the garden. She took a shawl and ran downstairs. Elizabeth was bubbling with relief, talking as she came.

"Oh he's gone! He was so smiling and peculiar, my father thinks he has bundled up the family silver and made off with it, and my mother is convinced he is pondering a proposal to Mary."

Charlotte directed their steps away from the house and responded in kind.

"He is not pondering a proposal to Mary for I have accepted his proposal to me, and I hope he has not made off with the family silver, because if he has, I could not possibly marry him. Do you think your father is serious?"

Elizabeth laughed aloud at this preposterous phantasy, put her hand quickly over her mouth and suddenly serious, looked at Charlotte wide eyed.

"You are funning?"

Charlotte, pink faced but smiling, shook her head.

"Oh Charlotte! What possessed you!"

Charlotte's affection for Elizabeth was deep. She hoped their friendship would not be a casualty to this strange turn of events in their lives.

"What possessed me was a sincere wish to be the wife of Mr. Collins, and I shall always be grateful to you Lizzie for refusing him."

Elizabeth strove to save her.

"Charlotte you of all people should not marry a stupid man."

"Why do you call him stupid?"

"We had decided he was not a sensible man even before we met him, when my father read us his letter. Charlotte, he actually urged my father to overlook the entail, claimed to be concerned at injuring his 'amiable' daughters and was anxious to make them every possible amends!" She laughed. "Really, even Jane was sceptical that he could make such atonement."

Charlotte was astonished. This sounded like a sincere approach to the healing of a family rift. He could hardly have made it plainer that he was seeking a wife. He had indeed been scorned. Elizabeth had not finished.

"And when we take him anywhere he is embarrassingly over affable and over complimentary. He cannot be sincere. And he is boastful, it's 'Lady Catherine' here and 'Lady Catherine' there. And you saw the exhibition he made of himself at Mr. Bingley's ball when he forced himself on Mr. Darcy."

Lizzie took Charlotte's hands into her own and looked her full in the eyes. Charlotte unable to recognize the man described as the man she had spoken with, and having seen nothing other than a brief courteous exchange at the ball, concluded that a generation of Bennet prejudice against the entail might prove impregnable. Unable to speak her thoughts she squeezed Lizzie's hand and smiled. Lizzie's response was a gaze of pure compassion.

"You mean it don't you? You really mean it. You are going to marry Mr. Collins. Oh Charlotte! I'm so sorry my father allowed him to come, so sorry." Then, with a sudden switch from compassion to curiosity, "How will you satisfy Lady Catherine? You know it was she who instructed him to find a wife?"

Speechless only for a second at this revelation, or perhaps, speculation, Charlotte responded with the truth.

"I shall discover that if and when I meet her."

After Elizabeth's departure Charlotte went in search of her father. He was with her mother and welcomed his daughter in expansive mood, eager to acquaint her with his assessment of Mr. Collins. She thought it prudent to inform him first of the forthcoming interview with Mr. Bennet, to which she had committed him. He agreed with her that a diplomatic visit from himself, although it might engender a coolness between the families, was preferable to the risk of a total sundering of all connection between Mr. Collins and his Bennet cousins should he attempt the task himself, but he was indignant. Lady Lucas was doubly indignant on his behalf, wondered how a fellow of two days acquaintance could cause such embarrassment between themselves and friends of a dozen years. Charlotte regretted her parents' anger, acknowledged that it was justified, as was the slighting reference to her beloved, but it did not diminish her happiness by one iota.

The embarrassing duty that she had laid on her father turned into a convivial visit. The ridiculous turn of events tickled Mr. Bennet's odd vein of humour and Sir William laughed with relief. They cast their eyes skyward and shook their heads at the extraordinary antics of Mr. Collins. Sir William confided that, apart from his eccentricities, he was a very satisfactory suitor for his daughter. Mr. Bennet conceded that although a neat draught of his cousin had proved challenging, generously diluted by the addition of Charlotte Lucas he may be tolerable, and perhaps in time, even palatable. They shared a celebratory glass from Mr. Bennet's decanter and Sir William went home smiling and victorious to his wife.

Lady Lucas was not so fortunate. Mrs. Bennet was piqued beyond endurance. She had let a son-in-law, eminently suitable for any one of her five daughters, slip though her fingers to be entrapped by the insufferable Charlotte Lucas, whom everybody knew was destined to be an old maid. As the friendship between the men grew warmer so the friendship between their wives cooled and Lady Lucas contrived in future never to be in the presence of her old friend unless Mr. Bennet was present also, to limit her loquacity on the subject of the forthcoming marriage.

7

Mr. Collins returned to Longbourn two weeks later. Since he had received a letter of congratulation and good wishes from Mr. Bennet, his deportment was not quite so sheepish as Mrs. Bennet would have liked. Allowing the minimum time to be spent on greetings, welcomes and thanks, he betook himself to Lucas Lodge in the highest spirits, to impart to Lady Lucas and her daughter the contents of a wonderful missive from his benefactress, Lady Catherine de Bourgh.

Lady Catherine, presuming a wedding at his church in Hunstan, had consulted her calendar and chosen the most convenient day. She would grace with her presence, both the ceremony and any gathering that might follow it. They could select one of the smaller salons at Rosings and consult with the Housekeeper about appropriate refreshment. He formally presented the precious document to Lady Lucas like an eager retriever dropping a plump partridge at her feet.

It touched Charlotte's heart but she knew it would not do. He turned his pleased face towards her and she permitted herself a slight smile and looked at her mother who was also smiling. Lady Lucas accepted the missive but left it unopened.

"Mr. Collins." She waved the document in her hand. "Lady Catherine is teasing you."

This statement from Lady Lucas was a revelation to Mr. Collins.

"She has a daughter does she not? She knows that no mother would allow anyone but herself to arrange a daughter's wedding." Mr. Collins looked uncertain about that. "We will consider any dates proposed and whatever the date we choose, Lady Catherine will, of course, be most welcome should she accept our invitation."

Lady Lucas quitted the room leaving Charlotte with her deflated betrothed.

"You had almost convinced us that Lady Catherine is perfect, it is reassuring to learn that she has a fault, and Presumption is not so very awful."

Mr. Collins was looking distinctly unsettled, but also thoughtful. She gave him a moment for the thought to mature then embarked on her own enterprise.

"Are you able to make a plan of your home and indicate to what use the rooms are put?" He beamed with pleasure, all awkwardness banished.

"I have anticipated you!"

He took from the small leather satchel, which was his constant companion, a piece of paper which he placed on a table and carefully unfolded, smoothing out the creases he offered to Charlotte a scale drawing of the ground floor of her future home. She gasped with delight and sat, entranced, as he gave her a guided tour from the front door through room after room and ante-room, and out at the rear. He produced a second paper with the same ceremony and laid before her the upper floor plan. As she watched the hands she had admired move, and heard his deep clear explaining voice, Charlotte filled with content.

"You did this for me?" She stroked the drawings gently. He nodded and indicated a third plan of the attics.

"Thank you. They are beautiful. You could not have given me a more welcome gift." She withdrew her gaze as his face grew pink. Her beloved, adept as he seemed to be at offering compliments, was a novice at receiving them.

The days of his visit were few. They walked into Meryton to look at the exterior of the house that had been her much loved home as a child, and was now her dowry. He pressed her hand and assured her that it would always be her own. They received, in the course of that walk, many good wishes from smiling acquaintances. Some of them remembered how high had once been her worth on the marriage market and most of them, courtesy of Mrs. Bennet, were aware that Miss Lucas was only Mr. Collins' second choice, he having been refused by her daughter Elizabeth; a revelation that neither diminished the common regard of Miss Lucas, nor enhanced that of Mrs. Bennet.

The Lucas's saw nothing of their friends at Longbourn during his visit, though compliments of each to the other were carried and delivered daily by Mr. Collins. All recognized that the uneasy atmosphere between them was inevitable, but would revert to normal in time. Since the cause of that unease, moving from cool indifference to warm welcome each morning and reluctant partings to cool greetings each evening, was Mr.Collins, this was a kind of justice. However, as he left eagerly every morning and returned ready for sleep each evening he did not suffer as much as Mrs. Bennet might have liked. Mr. Collins took back with him to Rosings a smaller, but no less elegant, missive from Lady Lucas for Lady Catherine. It ignored her Presumption but informed her of the date, time and place of the marriage and invited her to attend.

CHAPTER

8

Charlotte longed to be at Hunsford Parsonage and repeatedly unfolded and refolded the design of its ground and upper floors. She showed them to her mother who approved them without reservation. Lady Lucas enlightened her daughter as to her future husband's financial standing but admitted, as they sat together over tea cups, that she could not think of one single thing that she needed to mention about the competent running of an establishment, for Charlotte had long ceased to be an apprentice of that craft. She did wonder, however, if Charlotte might like to take the old recipe book with her to her new home. Charlotte accepted with a gasp of pleasure. This weighty shabby tome with years of neat entrances in her mother's hand was a gift indeed.

Lady Lucas's absolute confidence in her daughter concealed unexpressed misgivings about her future. She had no evidence of the good sense of the Reverend William Thomas Aston Collins, and deeply resented the presumptuous arrogance of Lady Catherine de Bourgh who seemed to be his idol. She felt it incumbent upon her to foster in Charlotte a confident self-reliance, and so reinforce her natural good sense. She did not conceal her own opinion of Lady Catherine.

Charlotte longed to be married but dreaded the embarrassment of a wedding arising out such strange circumstances. Since the two were inseparable, and her mother's ideas quite fixed, she resigned herself to any contingent disasters that might flow from herself and Mr. Collins jointly drawing attention to themselves. Her own apparel was the plainest Lady Lucas would allow though her younger sisters were frilled and rosetted. Lydia Bennet was heard to remark that her own mother looked more like a bride than did Charlotte Lucas. Mrs. Bennet demurred but looked pleased and Mr. Bennet, standing before the altar alongside his young cousin, was in no position to attempt any parental restraint.

Charlotte's worries proved needless. Her bridegroom looked smart and distinguished. Familiarity with the wedding ceremony gave his replies a confident ring and being the legitimate focus of attention proved a pleasure rather than an embarrassment. Finally, Mr. Bennet, not normally assiduous in guarding his family from ridicule, but adept at protecting himself from tedium, had demanded with a parental authority to see any speech the young man was proposing to make should the opportunity present itself. He had edited it by removing from it any reference to Lady Catherine except one in which he regretted her inability to be present. The speech was never made. At Charlotte's request, made with unusual firmness despite Lady Lucas's urging otherwise, the married couple eschewed the wedding breakfast and departed from the church door for an overnight visit to Thomas's old tutor, and then towards their future home, leaving celebration of the event to others.

Charlotte was not carried over the threshold of the Parsonage. She had forgotten that custom in her eagerness to enter and her husband seemed unaware of it. She followed the line his finger had taken on the precious piece of paper. Three of the rooms were heated by fires and in one of those a small circular table was dressed with cutlery and napery. In the scrubbed and shiny kitchen were the cook, and the house-maid who had admitted them. They bobbed a welcome and Thomas introduced them. She looked each one full in the face, and smiled and nodded, but did not speak. Beyond were pantry, larder, scullery, still-room, laundry with drying racks and rooms with cupboards to hold everything a household might need. She went out at the rear, followed a path which took her past a coach-house and round the house, looking into every window for a view of rooms she had visited. At the front door she entered for the second time and climbed the stairs, traversing again the rooms in the order in which he had pointed them out with his finger and coming once more to the head of the stairs.

She heaved a deep sigh, as though she had been holding her breath and turned to the face that had accompanied her throughout and was becoming so familiar. She saw pride and anxiety struggle for supremacy. Her silent concentration had unnerved him.

"What you have brought me to, my dear Thomas, is a little palace."

Pleasure and relief made his face handsome.

"Am I not fortunate in my patroness?"

Over-flowing with affection for both Thomas and the Parsonage she spontaneously stepped towards him and leaned her cheek against his chest. As his arms came round behind, not knowing how to purr, she sighed in deep content.

"Indeed you are." They stood for a blissful moment.

"If you put on your coat I will show you the church." Shocked, she stiffened and stepped back but only as far as the interlocked hands would allow. "Slipped your mind hadn't it?" He was laughing, a sincere laugh of real amusement. It had never been in her mind, she had been interested only in the Parsonage, what treason! He unlocked his hands. "Get your coat."

They turned left out of the Parsonage, crossed the wide lane that was a public way and walked to the left for a few yards passed a copse of tall trees and there, beyond a traditional lych-gate stood the church. It was almost a square, light in colour with a dark double front door and above the door on either side two very large windows with curved tops. They reflected the sunset back at them and inside the church the shadows of window panes lay on the pews and on the floor. Four more large windows, two on each side of the church set in white walls above shoulder-high wainscot, gave the best of the early evening light.

"Well windowed with good joinery." she said. "Gated pews and a musicians gallery." He indicated the wall behind her and there it was, over the doorway, she turned to look at it and smiled. As they walked down the aisle, passing the plain but somehow elegant pulpit on the right, it occurred to her for the first time that he might have *wanted* to be married here in his own church with people he knew, and felt a real pang of guilt at her thoughtless selfishness. She stroked the handsome wooden altar rail. "It is very beautiful Thomas. You are indeed fortunate in your patroness."

As the evening drew to a close it seemed to Charlotte that Thomas, in an easy chair opposite her in the small sitting room, had heaved a sigh of relief, shed everything about him that had seemed awkward and ungainly, and settled back gratefully into the place where he most longed to be. Fancifully she thought of him as a knight who had reluctantly but boldly left his castle to undertake a quest for a wife; challenged to encounter and overcome any dangerous entrapments laid to frustrate him. He had triumphed and returned with a bride. Her fanciful musings buckled somewhat at this point. His bride was not young and beautiful, and she had not been his first choice. Had she, herself, not laid an entrapment? He was absorbed in correspondence that had awaited his return and she was able to gaze on him, unobserved, as she had done in the shrubbery at Longbourn. She sighed with deep content and his head raised with an inquiring look; his face could look very pleased without actually smiling, she liked that. Her answer was a contented nod, happy that they could communicate without words. She was deeply penitent that she had given no thought to St. Andrew's Church but she did love its Parson very dearly, and plain common sense told Charlotte that, in itself, had made her a bride worth winning.

CHAPTER

9

Charlotte was nervous but determined as she ventured into the park next morning on her way to Rosings to find Lady Catherine de Bourgh. The devastating quandary in which she found herself must be resolved. The day was bright but cold, following an unexpected overnight frost. She wanted to walk quickly, as in an emergency, but the path would not permit it. She slowed her pace, strove to quiet her agitated mind.

The three days since the wedding had been both joyful and sad. They had paid an overnight visit to Mr. Collins' old tutor, the Reverend Beevers, with whom he had made his home in the years preceding his entry to Oxford, and whose example he had followed in taking Holy Orders. The older man and his man-servant had been welcoming and attentive, spontaneously affectionate and eager to discover more of his adventures since last seen. They had commented, almost paternally, on his growth, appearance, maturity, and not least his good fortune in discovering and marrying Charlotte. She liked Mr. Beevers very much, and he had presented them with two carved prie-dieux as a wedding present.

Since Mr. Beevers had mentioned that their journey to the parsonage would take them past his childhood home she had prevailed upon Thomas to let her see it, though he had been very reluctant. He had gasped with surprise when he saw it. It was a small Tudor mansion, now in the loving care of a stranger, but clearly not as he remembered

PEGGY TULIP

it. Charlotte urged him to make himself known but he refused. The visit made him withdrawn. She had deliberately rendered her own life transparent to him at their first meeting but she knew nothing of his former life, apart from the fact that he had told her father that both his parents had died. She suppressed curiosity, reasoning that there was a lifetime to discover all, and felt her excitement grow as every moment brought them closer to Hunsford Parsonage, the new home that she already loved. When she saw the pale stone exterior and they had traced the familiar route through the rooms within it, she knew that a more fortunate or happier bride had never existed.

This morning was the first separation since their marriage. They each had duties to perform. Thomas had set about his with an easy familiarity, and an eagerness to re-tread his old steps with his new status. Charlotte, with a thrill of pleasurable anticipation, had nodded smiling into her looking glass, acknowledging the mistress of Hunsford Parsonage in her first establishment. She had then gone to engage properly with her cook, to congratulate her on the excellent meal that had welcomed them home and open a discussion on future catering. She had been aghast to discover that the servants at the parsonage were not her own but Lady Catherine de Bourgh's, and that Mrs. Fountain, Housekeeper at Rosings, was housekeeper of both establishments. This revelation had fallen like a cold stone on her heart, and had left both the cook and herself in a state of real embarrassment.

She had left the kitchen, which was not her kitchen, for the bedroom that no longer felt like her bedroom, and stared out of the window onto the lane that led to Rosings. This was a blow she had never anticipated, a situation of which she had never heard. It would not do. She said the words aloud. "It will not do."

She had taken a chair to the window. There was not a soul in sight, just the trees and the lane and evidence of an unexpected overnight frost and a watery sun. She must be mistress of her own establishment, it was the fulfilment of her life's ambition, not to be so was unthinkable. She needed her mother's advice but could not delay to obtain it. To whom could she turn? It could only be to Lady Catherine de Bourgh, whom she knew she must respect but by whom, her mother had warned, she must not be over-awed. She could not delay until she saw Thomas. She feared he would tell her that she must submit, when he could not possibly know what that sacrifice would demand of her. She had to take her chance with Lady Catherine. There was no alternative.

She re-dressed with special care and set off while her resolution was high. After a few minutes walking, her spirits rose in the bright fresh air and her pace quickened as she approached the curve in the path. Rosings, as pink as its name promised, coming into view beyond the boles of giant trees, took her breath away. It was more vast than anything she had imagined. A warm pink image framed at the edges and the windows with palest stone that seemed to gleam white in the morning sunshine. A groom, leading a horse past its white colonnaded portico seemed like a midget. She stopped. Her resolution crumbled in an instant. She tore her gaze away from the sight, and stumbled aside into a small glade.

She failed to notice the beauty of the place until she reached, and sat on a marble bench. There were patches of frost still in the grass and there were huge mature trees. The watery yellow sun shining through the head of one of them, outlined a myriad tiny twigs and twiglets into a delicate black lace. It was beautiful but it was melancholy and it matched her mood. She was completely over-awed, and not even by Lady Catherine de Bourgh, merely by the size of her house.

She stared at the remains of frost in the grass, at the trunks and boughs of the great trees, at the low morning sun that troubled her eyes and drew a glow from the marble bench on which she sat, at the black and gold lace of twigs and sunshine. It was beautiful but she could not bear it and closed her eyes.

Charlotte Lucas had not shed many tears in her life, and never a tear of despair. Charlotte Collins, isolated, overwrought, beset, humbled and frustrated, did so on the fourth day after her marriage. They burst from her, loud and uncontrollable, where there was no one to hear and until there were no more to shed and her sobs became deep gasping breaths.

The outburst left her exhausted and helpless, without the will even to return to the parsonage of which she was not the mistress. She drew herself inward, away from the creeping cold and tears seeped again from under her closed eyelids. She abandoned herself, shivering and hunched, to a misery she could never have imagined.

From somewhere very deep Charlotte felt the comfort of her mother's hand on her shoulder, come to arouse her out of a dark place. She waited, soothed, for the familiar voice to call her and offer some characteristic stimulating observation. The hand moved, she was taken firmly, with two hands by the shoulders, but the voice that spoke was not her mother's voice. The voice of a woman was asking persistently for "Mrs. Collins! Mrs. Collins!" She opened her eyes.

"Mrs. Collins. I fear you are not well. Shall I send someone to find your husband?"

"No!" She cried in alarm. "Please no! Do not do that!"

She tried to rise but her limbs were numb, she could not stand and collapsed helpless onto the bench. The slow tears of misery became rushing tears of embarrassment. She was a spectacle!

"I brought a cloak." She felt the weight of the cloak as it was lowered onto her shoulders and arranged around and over her knees. The woman sat alongside and took both of Charlotte's hands into her own warm hands and gently exercised them as she spoke calmly over the sounds of sobbing that Charlotte was helpless to control.

"Ethel saw you sit as she came to the house. These benches are not suitable for days like this. I was concerned at the delay. I shall stay until you feel a little stronger then I will leave you again, only for short a time to arrange for a carriage."

"No! Please no! I will not have a carriage!" Charlotte rose again and stood, unstable but determined; but she could not stop the tears. "I cannot bear to be so foolish."

"You are not foolish, Mrs. Collins. You are very chilled and you are distressed, and both can be relieved. If you will raise your chin I can button the cloak, there, now I shall take your elbow and give you support as we walk to the House. The walk will warm you a little and aid your recovery. It is a short distance. I am Mary Fountain, Housekeeper at Rosings. I know that Lady Catherine would wish me to make you welcome and to give any assistance that you require. Are you sure you do not want to be carried?"

"Quite sure!"

Charlotte, trembling, and in considerable discomfort but determined to walk, was guided by the woman who had buttoned her into the cloak, towards the rosy brick building with a myriad twinkling glass windows that trumpeted the wealth and power of Lady Catherine de Bourgh. They did not go to the mighty doorway with the columns but to a less stately doorway at the side of the house. She was relieved of the cloak and of her own coat and bonnet by enchanted hands, like a child in a fairy tale, and led into a warm sitting room. There, exhausted, she collapsed gratefully into chair to one side of a fire and closed her eyes. A shawl was lain over her shoulders, a rug over her legs and a footstool set beneath her feet. A cup was placed on a small table by her side.

"Drink, Mrs. Collins. Hot chocolate, it is a very comforting beverage."

Charlotte thought her hands could not lift the cup. The woman had spoken and acted with kindness, but her authority oppressed Charlotte. She expressed her thanks in a voice so small that it did not seem her own and closed her eyes again, grateful that the tears had ceased at last.

"I shall leave you for a few minutes to rest and warm through. No-one will disturb you until I return."

Charlotte, small and ashamed, sat tense and unmoving behind closed eyelids and listened to the shifting of the fire, the ticking of a clock and her own shallow breaths. After a few minutes she lifted the cup with unsteady tingling hands and warmed them as she drank. She replaced the cup carefully, wrapped her hands in the shawl and stared at the fire as it flickered and settled. The ticking clock and the flickering fire were comforting, and her breaths were calmer. She relaxed, breathed deeply, acknowledged her disgraceful collapse into helplessness and regretted the rash act that had brought it about. It would have been wiser to be acquainted with Lady Catherine de Bourgh before being so determined not to be overawed. She *was* overawed, and merely by the size of her house! Her cause, however, was right. Lady Catherine was a usurper. Indignation stiffened her. She threw off the shawl and the rug. It was the duty and occupation of a married woman to oversee the running of the household. Proposals of marriage were made and accepted on that understanding. She knew this to be true. Unfortunately, it seemed a truth with which Thomas was unacquainted. She had to make clear to him what had been her expectation – indeed the expectation of any woman accepting a proposal of marriage – and just hope that he could find the resolution to restore her happiness. These were the conclusions she was sharing with the fire when the opening door brought her back to the present. As Mrs. Fountain entered Charlotte rose to her feet.

"Ah, Mrs. Collins, I can see at once that you have recovered. A little warmth can work wonders."

"A little warmth and a very great deal of patient kindness, Mrs. Fountain." Charlotte was surprised to find that the handsome smiling woman with dark eyes and dark hair, was much younger and more slight than she had seemed to be. "I am deeply grateful to you. Please forgive me for making such an exhibition of myself. I am very ashamed."

Mrs. Fountain gestured that Charlotte should sit again, and then sat opposite to her.

"There was no exhibition Mrs. Collins I can assure you of that, but you were very distressed and in some physical danger. I have no wish to embarrass you, or to intrude upon your personal life, but could I help if knew the cause? I promise total discretion."

Charlotte was momentarily still. Serendipity; the word and concept had been a gift to her by one of her best tutors years ago but never, she thought, quite so opportune as now. The debacle in pursuit of one usurper had brought her, extraordinarily, into sympathetic union with the second. She smiled into the face of Mrs. Fountain and explained that she had expected to be the mistress of the Parsonage and discovered the shocking truth that she was not. She had further discovered that she lacked the courage to attempt a persuasion of Lady Catherine to remedy that situation, because she had been over-awed by the size of her house. Mrs. Fountain was looking at her in astonishment.

"Mrs. Collins, you have misunderstood, or perhaps been unwittingly misled. The present arrangement is simply an indulgence granted by Lady Catherine to Mr. Collins for his greater convenience. Your presence provides what the Parsonage previously lacked, a Mistress who would engage the servants of her choice."

Charlotte was silent, absorbing the significance of what she heard.

"Oh Mrs. Fountain! If I had not been overawed by Rosings I would have forced myself on Lady Catherine only to sound like a babbling idiot."

"You could not have forced yourself upon her because she is not here. She is due to return in two weeks." She continued, choosing her words carefully. "She is quite awesome. For the purposes of persuasion I approach her from the left, two feet away and slightly to the rear. She hears more acutely with her left ear, but," she dropped her voice to a whisper, "I attempt nothing when her countenance is pink." The smile broadened. "I strongly advise you that if you seek anything of Lady Catherine, to do it through your husband, she is always willing to give her attention to Mr. Collins."

Charlotte lost no time in sending a letter to her mother, and Lady Lucas rearranged her immediate engagements, persuaded her husband to allow her the coach for three days and set off for the Parsonage.

CHAPTER

11

Thomas seemed not to understand Charlotte's question when she asked if he had found the servants satisfactory. He did mention that the cook made an excellent cold meat pie. His answers to further questions about his parsonage were quite clear. Nothing in it belonged to him. Everything was here when he first saw the Parsonage, except the two prie-dieux, delivered this morning by a carrier and now standing alongside each other by their bedroom wall. He had brought only himself, his clothes and his books and chattels, all delivered by the same carrier who had brought the prie-dieux.

Charlotte was rehearsing questions she thought Lady Lucas would ask. She had longed for her mother to see her new home but the presumption of Lady Catherine had so affronted Lady Lucas that she had declared she could not visit the Parsonage because even an accidental meeting with that lady was more than she could countenance. Lady Catherine's absence was a gift.

Lady Lucas was won over by the pleasing site and generous exterior of the parsonage. Descending from her coach at the small gate she was greeted by a son-in-law, almost at ease with her on his own territory, extending his right hand. She took the hand firmly in both of hers, greeted him warmly, and bringing her daughter's hand also into the embrace, wished them happiness in their first home and requested a speedy entry to the house to escape the cold gusty breezes.

An hour later mother and daughter sat with their heads over a pot of tea and two cups. Lady Lucas opined that the house had been both renovated and extended quite recently; it had been fitted and furnished with good taste and no little expense to meet all the basic needs of a household.

"Am I not fortunate in my patroness? That is what he said to me." Said Charlotte. Lady Lucas pursed her lips in distaste.

"Yes." She had been impressed. "I agree that he is fortunate, very fortunate." She spoke guardedly. "But she is not *your* patroness." She made her point by extending an impolite finger towards her daughter. "Never forget it."

Charlotte had decided that she needed nothing from Lucas Lodge but her small writing desk, which her mother had thoughtfully brought, and the cheval looking-glass from her bedroom. Lady Lucas suggested that the house lacked a supply of superior linen, silver, glass and china. Since Charlotte already owned some of these things, should she not have them to hand? Would Charlotte like her to arrange their removal? Charlotte thought not. She would unpack them herself first, alone and joyfully, at Lucas Lodge. She tried to remember what they were.

"Will I still like those things I wonder?"

"You will have to like them Charlotte, you chose them."

She smiled with pleasure at her new name and address on the cards her mother had brought, but was alarmed when Lady Lucas suggested that Mr. Collins should provide a list of those households upon which it would be appropriate to leave one of Charlotte's cards, and one of her own. Tomorrow, her mother had decided, would be a suitable day for leaving their cards. Charlotte expressed her doubts at such an enterprise.

"My Dear, you are going amongst these people for the first time and will be amongst them for many years. It will be to your advantage for them to know from the beginning that you are a person of consequence. My card will bestow that consequence."

Lady Lucas was behaving as she always behaved, with the good sense and quick decisions that Charlotte admired, but she was doing it in Charlotte's establishment and the daughter realized how much she had grown away from her mother and towards her husband in the short time since her marriage. The thought pleased her and she was smiling on her mother when she spoke, softly but firmly.

"No." This unusual word startled Lady Lucas. "It is not an appropriate thing to ask of a parson to select *parishioners* for his wife to call upon."

Lady Lucas was silenced.

"I do have a friend who might do it." Charlotte lied, but did so in the hope and expectation that Mary Fountain would indeed become her friend. "We could walk to Rosings this afternoon and ask her."

"I cannot go to Rosings."

"Lady Catherine is not there. That is why you agreed to visit us."

"I cannot enter her house. It would be an impertinence."

"I shall go this afternoon without you. Have you brought your silks?"

"I never go anywhere without them."

Husband, wife and mother-in-law met cordially at mid-day, enjoyed a genial light meal and dispersed to their several occupations. Lady Lucas took a chair by the fire in the small sitting room, to recover from the rigours of her journey and to pursue artistic perfection for utilitarian ends as she worked new seat covers for existing dining chairs. Charlotte went on an expedition to Rosings.

The strengthening wind had turned cold and blustery. Charlotte secured a shawl over her coat, selected sturdy boots and a close bonnet and set off to discuss matters with Mrs. Fountain.

The tree boughs protested at the wind as leaves were dragged off and tumbled indiscriminately. The strings chafed her chin as the swirling gusts filled the small brim of her bonnet. She stopped at the marble bench, removed the bonnet and secured the shawl tightly about her head, neck and shoulders, then moved on with the bonnet dancing and swivelling from where it hung on her arm. The panelled doors of Rosings were shut and piles of garden debris swirled and rose and fell under the colonnaded portico. The wind ceased buffeting as she passed the corner of the house and entered the side door. The only person present was a maid carrying a coal scuttle. She was opening the door of the room that Charlotte knew.

"I'm looking for Mrs. Fountain!" Charlotte called hurriedly before the door could close. The girl put down the scuttle carefully, walked to the outside doorway collecting Charlotte by a handful of shawl as she went. Out of the door she pointed to the back of the building.

"Down there," she said, with the friendliest of smiles. "Round the corner, in the door. There's a room with a man in it." She gave an encouraging push and a pat and returned to her duties.

Charlotte, unfamiliar with the dialect, momentarily at a loss, was stunned when she realized what had happened. She could not bear to believe that one of Lady Catherine's maids had taken her for a servant. Her feet knew not which way to turn. Back to the parsonage, never to come again to this dreadful place where a visit turned her into a fool? Blessing her mother and steeling her resolve, she took from her bag one of the cards she had brought and returned to the room where the maid was transferring coals from the scuttle to a copper box.

"Ah. That was quick." She said consolingly, putting down the tongs.

"Will you take this please? Give it to Mrs. Fountain and tell her I am here." Charlotte removed her shawl as she spoke.

The girl made no move to take the card. She stood motionless with her mouth open and stared at Charlotte who could not believe that she could be the cause of such alarm in any human being.

"It was a misunderstanding." She spoke softly. "What is your name?"

"Dorcas Ma'am."

"Now Dorcas, this is my card. Let Mrs. Fountain know that I am here." Without reply Dorcas took the card, bobbed and fled.

Disconcerted by the strange turn of events, Charlotte tried to concentrate on why she was here. She had come to sound out Mrs. Fountain on the topic of servants, on the ownership of furnishings in the parsonage, and whether she might know suitable recipients for visiting cards. She took a seat and rehearsed these matters. As she was doing this, the clock that had comforted her on the previous occasion chimed the quarter. She rose, over warm, removed her outdoor clothes and laid them over the back of a sofa. She saw her reflection in a glazed picture and gave some attention to her dishevelled hair. She took a cursory glance at some small landscape and seascape paintings then, when she reached them again having circled the room, studied them more closely. When the clock struck a further quarter she looked longingly at her coat and bonnet and, but for possible repercussions on the long vanished Dorcas, would have dressed herself and left the premises. She was looking again, at pictures behind the door, when it opened towards her and a humming footman entered and made for the fireplace. He picked up the tongs to refuel the fire and stopped when he noticed the unfinished chore of Dorcas. When Charlotte tried to offer some explanation, he leaped round with a cry of alarm and dropped the tongs with a clatter onto the hearth. Mrs. Fountain, rather breathless, came quickly through the open door followed closely by Dorcas, panting with sobs.

"Good afternoon, Mrs. Collins. I am very sorry you have been kept waiting. William, when you finish what you are doing, please take Mrs. Collins' coat. Dorcas remove the coal scuttle please. Explain to Mrs. Peggs how you have spent your time, and ask her to provide tea for Mrs. Collins and myself."

Mrs. Fountain's modulated voice reduced the discord to harmony. The door closed silently behind William and Mrs. Fountain indicated with her hand.

"I think we might call that *your* chair Mrs. Collins."

"What did I do that was so wrong?" It was the question of a bewildered child. Mrs. Fortune sat opposite, smiling.

"Not wrong. Unfortunate. You came in the wrong door."

"But it was the door you brought me to...."

"On that occasion discretion demanded it. That door is not attended, it is used by those who come and go regularly. The other misfortune was that you happened upon someone least able to do what you required. I came across her, by accident, while she was seeking me in a house she hardly knows, with a card in her hand that she could not read."

The words carried a reprimand but the voice did not. Charlotte put her brow in the palm of her hand and suffered for the unfortunate Dorcas.

"Can I apologize to Dorcas?"

Mrs. Fountain nodded in pleased surprise. "Yes. May I deliver it to her as a message on your behalf? She will appreciate it, she is a good kind girl from a very nice family."

"Please tell her I am really sorry. Her first instructions were sound," said Charlotte, and told what they had been, "If I had followed them I would have.."

"You would have embarrassed your husband Mrs. Collins. You would have embarrassed yourself and you would have embarrassed me. You should have found me through the services of a footman at the front door."

A footman brought a tea tray and Charlotte considered those sentences as tea was poured. She had accepted that Thomas might embarrass *her*. She had forgiven him in advance. That she might prove an embarrassment to him, herself or anyone else was alarming.

"It is a very large door," she said by way of appeasement, "and it was shut."

"Even the largest doors are made to open, Mrs. Collins, otherwise they would not be doors."

The doors did open: and close.

After a conference on Parsonage Furniture, (all of which belonged to the Parsonage); Servants, (Mrs. Collins was at liberty to employ the existing servants or to seek others as she wished); and Parish Visits, (Mrs. Fountain felt sufficiently familiar with the area to indicate some who were likely to welcome a friendly visit from the parson's wife.) However, she would be cautious of visiting cards, because she could not be confident of literacy.

At the end of a useful companiable meeting, Mrs. Fountain, informed that the now turbulent winds carried spasmodic rain and sleet, had commanded a covered carriage for Mrs. Collins. Charlotte, deeply embarrassed, had stood in her coat and bonnet in a vast entrance hall with marble floors and columns. Alongside her was Mrs. Fountain, also in cloak and bonnet, carrying Charlotte's shawl to tuck round her once she was in the carriage. Charlotte had protested as far as politeness allowed but Mrs. Fountain had insisted that Lady Catherine would wish it. The doors were opened for Charlotte. Before she could step through them, Lady Lucas's carriage with Lady Lucas and Mr. Collins aboard, arrived to claim her. The ensuing fandango of horses, coaches and coachmen facing in opposite directions and wishing to turn about in limited space, atrocious conditions and fading light was not to be resolved at speed. Lady Lucas and Mr. Collins entered the house and the doors were closed.

Mrs. Fountain led them all back to the warm drawing room now familiar to Charlotte, provided hot chocolate and withdrew, promising to let them know when their carriage was ready. Charlotte, delighted that she had found a wise and kindly friend, was sorry that her mother could not be further acquainted with the Housekeeper and told her so. Lady Lucas, fatigued by the rough and tumble of events and displeased at her enforced entry to Rosings, the grandeur of which had impressed her more than she liked to admit, was unsympathetic. She drew her daughter away from the hearing of her husband who was studying a picture as he slowly savoured his chocolate.

"She cannot be your friend Charlotte. She is a servant."

The party from the parsonage was not long delayed and they embarked from the more sheltered side-entrance. The buffeting of the horses and then of the coach as they left the shelter of the house caused concern that the coach might blow over but the short journey was accomplished safely and horses and humans were secured from wind and sleet.

Sleep evaded Charlotte then came fitfully but asleep or awake her mind was filled with thoughts and images of Dorcas, upon whom she had unwittingly inflicted an impossible task, or of the entirely admirable Mary Fountain who could not be her friend because she was a servant.

She woke from a more restful sleep later in the morning to an empty room; Thomas had been summoned away at dawn.

CHAPTER

13

Charlotte and Lady Lucas were in the drawing room overlooking the lane to Rosings. Charlotte had taken a chair that gave her a clear view of the Parsonage gate. She held a novel in her hand but her agitated mind had given it scant attention. The afternoon was advancing as she waited for the return of Thomas, whom she had not yet seen that day. He had been aroused before she was awake to go to the bedside of an elderly widow in the hamlet of Hutton. Lady Lucas in a chair by the fire, cushion on her lap, frame on the cushion, skeins of silk thread to hand, concentrated on the perfection of each stitch in her creation. They had been thus since their mid-day meal.

The house was quiet. The world outside was still, as if recovering from the excesses of the previous night when the gusts that had plucked at Charlotte's bonnet and then gained the strength to challenge Lady Lucas's coach, had by the early hours of the morning cast off all restraint and burst headlong in a deadly curving swathe around the countryside. The parsonage was unscathed but at Rosings the wind had dragged over a great tree whose bare roots stood taller than a man. Over the surrounding area the gale had toppled lesser trees, pushed over chimneys, torn up mature thatch and caused more than one well-built haystack to lean perilously. There seemed to have been no direct casualties, humanity at that time being mostly abed.

It was astonishing to Charlotte that they were so well informed and it was due entirely to Molly, Lady Lucas's maid who aided by Ethel the parlour maid, had skilfully gleaned and shared all information from passers-by on road and lane. Charlotte had known Molly for a dozen years but never before seen her perform this service.

Conversation had been desultory. Lady Lucas had paused her stitching and raised her head to opine that, on reflection, she thought that indicating suitable persons on whom his wife might make a social call was in no way inappropriate for a parson. Charlotte, with a list from Mrs. Fountain of those whom she felt would appreciate a call, agreed, and said she would discuss it with him. She did not mention that Mrs. Fountain could not answer for their literacy and had warned against visiting cards.

She had been grateful for her mother's disinclination for conversation as she wrestled with the demons of misfortune that had entrapped her on her two visits to Rosings. She was the black kitten in her father's warehouse, dropped into a strange place and licked mercilessly into submission. She felt a need for confession to those whom she feared she had disgraced, her husband and her mother, but knew she could not confess to either of them. She felt that Mary Fountain had given her a kind of absolution. The Housekeeper had witnessed and delivered her from total humiliation on two occasions, but her mother said it was not possible to have a friendship with her because she was a servant. She was heart-sick for the innocent Dorcas. That child's tribulation had been much worse than her own.

They were brought to attention by a knock at the door. Molly was almost bursting.

"A caller on horseback going down to Rosings Ma'am, passed Reverend Collins back down the road less than half a mile, with a child in a sling on his front, coming very slow."

The explosive news brought both women to their feet. Cushion, frame, silks and book tumbled to the floor. Stable hands were mustered to meet and aid Mr. Collins. The ladies at the window watched them go. Lady Lucas's groom returned carrying the child. She was taken by

Molly and laid, at Lady Lucas's instruction, upon her lap. She was little more than a baby, wrapped in a soot-stained rug, light haired, dressed in night clothes and very dirty. Eyes and lips protested weakly before she lapsed back into sleep. Lady Lucas requested a shawl of Ethel. Charlotte watched as Thomas waited at the gate, his back bent double on his horse while the sling around him and various parcels and packages tied to him and the saddle were untied and removed, making it possible for the men to help him dismount. She watched as they half walked, half carried him into the house and lowered him groaning onto a comfortable chair in the drawing room. He closed his eyes and asked for a slice of cook's meat pie and a tankard of ale. It was some time before his aching arms and numbed hands could handle either, then he ate three slices from a tray on his lap, groaning softly and wincing at intervals as his tortured body readjusted itself.

The refreshment revived him somewhat. He had not been summoned to Hutton for a death, but to a house that had been half demolished when a falling chimney shattered the roof. Its owner, Mrs. Allen, had summoned him urgently because she must remove at once to the home of her son and must relinquish the care of the child back to its mother. The mother was Mrs. Fountain. Mrs. Allen had understood the arrangement to be covert, but she had no alternative but to involve another party. She had asked Mr. Collins to take the child and her belongings to her mother at Rosings. Charlotte found her own astonished look met by a look of equal astonishment from her mother.

Thomas proposed to rest until he recovered the use of his limbs then walk to Rosings in the expectation of returning with Mrs. Fountain. His words became barely audible as his head rested on the back of his chair and he gently went to sleep.

Charlotte and her mother sat in the quiet drawing room, looking in turn on the sleeping Thomas and the sleeping child.

"Well!" said Lady Lucas after a long silence. "Who? Why? How? What?"

"I cannot even speculate."

"One cannot but speculate," said Lady Lucas, "about a concealed child."

Charlotte's heart squeezed as she thought with affection of Mary Fountain.

"I think we need a cup of tea," said Lady Lucas. Charlotte rose with relief at something to do and walked to the kitchen where she found Mrs. Fountain, cloaked with her hood back, asking urgently to see Mr. Collins, her face tortured by anxiety. The need for tea forgotten she took her by the elbow and guided her to the drawing room, speaking as they went. "I'm afraid he has fallen asleep," and then as Mrs. Fountain hesitated. "I am certain he would wish me to waken him."

Mrs. Fountain stopped when she saw her daughter on Lady Lucas's lap. Lady Lucas watched her face transform with relief.

"Oh Lady Lucas!" She said no more but gave her a look of deep gratitude. She looked at the face of her child, deep in sleep and sighed, then looked sympathetically at the sleeping Thomas. She whispered.

"Do not wake him. The groom who passed him on the road told me what agonies your husband must have suffered. You must know that I can never be sufficiently grateful."

"He needs to speak to you."

Thomas woke the moment Charlotte touched him and was instantly alert and astonished to see Mrs. Fountain before him.

"Mrs. Fountain!" He tried to rise but found it difficult. He indicated a chair for her and continued when she was seated. "Mrs. Allen was most anxious that you should know that she saw no alternative but to send your daughter to you. A falling chimney and broken roof opened the house to the elements. Wet soot and plaster were everywhere, even...." He indicated Lady Lucas and she lifted the clean shawl that wrapped the soot spattered child. Mrs. Fountain covered her mouth for a moment with a hand. "The house is uninhabitable."

"And Mrs. Allen?"

"Very shocked but unhurt. She goes to her son. She was awaiting his coach."

"Thank God! She is a very good woman. She has become my greatest friend. What of Annie, the nursemaid?"

"Shocked but unharmed. She has gone back to her mother."

Mrs. Fountain looked at each of them in turn. "Thank you for the kindness you have shown, I am sure each of you will know how deeply grateful I am."

"But who told you?" asked Thomas. "Who knew other than myself?"

"The man who spoke to you on the road was a groom from Rosings. He recognized you. Lady Lucas, may I borrow the shawl?"

"You will take her to Rosings?" Lady Lucas tightened the shawl around the child and the sleeping burden changed hands.

"I have a small carriage outside, and a cot is being prepared," Mrs. Fountain smiled at Charlotte, "by Dorcas."

Lady Lucas had a premonition.

"Will this storm bring Lady Catherine home?"

"A messenger left for London early this morning with news of the storm. I think she will consider it a duty to return immediately."

Thomas managed to rise and, putting aside protests, opened the door to escort mother and daughter to the carriage, Charlotte moved towards them.

"What is your daughter's name?"

Mrs. Fountain looked into Charlotte's eyes, with humour.

"Charlotte! I call her Lottie." She paused for a considerable time as if wondering whether to continue, and then did so, speaking softly. "She is named for her father, Charles. He was a Major in the 95th Rifles. He died early in the retreat to La Coruna. He never saw her, she is a posthumous child."

She passed through the door with Thomas and it closed behind them. Charlotte looked, through sudden tears, at her mother, also moist eyed who had her fingers over her mouth and spoke through them.

"Oh how tragic! What a brave woman."

They were a subdued trio. The perilous retreat, the astonishing victory at Corunna, and the death of the commander-in-chief had moved the Nation and then slipped from memory. The pathos of the posthumous child brought it back.

Lady Lucas to avoid any possibility, however remote, of meeting Lady Catherine decided to leave early next morning. She remembered some of the things she had intended to discover during her visit, and felt that the strange turn of events made this a suitable time for intimacy.

"And you, Thomas," she said softly addressing him, with familiarity, for the first time by his Christian name. "Tell me about your mother. Did she die when you were young?"

Mr. Collins started, "Yes," he said and raised a hand. "Excuse me." He rose without too much difficulty and left the room.

"Oh Mother!"

"Charlotte, that was not an improper question."

Charlotte followed him. He was in the bedroom removing a small flat wooden box from his leather satchel. He opened the lid and watching her closely, gave her a small silver framed portrait of a young woman with fair curling hair and deep blue eyes.

"Your mother?"

"Yes."

"Thomas, thank you. She is so beautiful. I can show it to her?"

"Of course."

Lady Lucas was attempting to untangle skeins of silk that had fallen earlier from her lap. She put them down as Charlotte offered her the likeness.

"This is Thomas's mother."

"What a beautiful girl!" She gazed on it then looked up. "He has her eyes. I remarked them the first time I saw him."

Their wedding gifts from Mr. Beevers stood in their bedroom, at a comfortable angle for their eyes to meet after prayer. Charlotte had been as delighted by the gift as a child with a special toy. She had never seen such a thing and suspected it was papist, which made it rather exciting.

Her prayers this evening included one for Mary Fountain and her child and she raised her head to find Thomas's blue eyes upon her, as she had come to expect. She told him she had noticed that his evening prayers were very brief. His responding smile was mischievous.

"The Third Collect. 'Lighten our darkness we beseech thee, O Lord; and by thy great mercy defend us from all perils and dangers of this night'.

She smiled back. "Why do you keep your mother in a box?" The reply seemed to require deep thought.

"That was how it was given to me. I was told not to let anyone see it, lest it was taken from me."

"Who gave it to you?"

"Anne."

"Who was she?" He shook his head very ruefully.

"I wish I knew. If she ever told me I've forgotten. But she was wonderful, and she was urgent about the picture. 'Always keep it close Tom, or you may lose it.' So I have."

"She called you Tom? That is a term of affection."

"She took an interest in me."

"Was she old?" He shook his head.

"No. She sometimes brought her son, about my size. She died though; I remember it was dreadful. I was just turned five, at my first school with a kindly woman called Mrs. Adams. There were four boys. We lived with her and she taught us."

Charlotte, eyes pricking suddenly with tears, remembered her own brother at that age, the pride and noisy nuisance at the heart of the Lucas family. She felt a sudden tenderness for the mysterious Anne, quickly said another prayer and resisted the longing to question him further.

15

Lady Lucas was off betimes the next morning. Thomas, somewhat stiff, left soon afterwards to join others for an inspection of the church. Charlotte was piqued. She resented her mother's premature departure and Thomas's evident delight in the imminent return of Lady Catherine irked her. She looked from the drawing-room window onto the lane that led to Rosings where there was an irritating amount of coming and going.

She decided to indulge herself in a tour of her establishment. She simply moved from room to room in a leisurely manner, taking a different seat to enjoy a different aspect, looking out of windows to refresh her memory of the view. It was an exercise which soothed her. From an upstairs window she noticed for the first time, beyond the lane to Rosings, a smaller footway not visible from the ground floor windows. It appeared to run along the edge of the estate, separated from the public road by hedging and trees. It was a long way from Rosings.

Very soon, warmly clad and well shod, the Parsonage behind her, she was picking her way through leaves and twigs forced off the trees by the storm. The trees, tall and slender, rose from grass on either side of the path. The fallen leaves were pale yellow. She heard the calling of men's voices far to the right, the sounds clear but not the words and from somewhere, the steady thrust and heave of a two-man saw. The path was little used and she moved forward cautiously. There were potentially hazardous lumps under the leaves. She retrieved a stick from one of them and used it to poke at the others. Her lungs filled with cool air smelling of damp earth. Exercise and fresh air raised her spirits and she moved forward confidently into the trees as the sounds faded behind her. When her stick snapped she turned and looked back. The Parsonage was not in sight, the path had curved.

She paused and her thoughts turned to Mrs. Fountain and the events of last evening. Intrigued by her strange and surprising history, she felt even more strongly the pull of friendship. She had really wanted to offer a home to Lottie but the presence of her mother had restrained her. Suddenly, a thunderous pounding and terrifying cry from she knew not where, drove Charlotte from her deep reverie to instant panic. Spinning to confront the terror she stumbled on a tussock of grass at the path edge and falling forward maintained her balance by embracing a tree. Winded and confused she held on to it.

"It was a coach!" A tall energetic young man in a buttoned up caped-coat and a hat pulled firmly onto his brow was hastening towards her from further up the small lane. When he was level he extended a hand to rescue her.

"Coach?"

He put a finger to his lips and a cupped hand to his ear in the direction of the drive to Rosings. She heard, beyond the trees, horses' hooves and a wail.

"A horn!"

"I'm afraid so."

He seemed to be apologizing. His face, the hat removed, was pleasant, weathered and strong featured. He retained a supporting hand on her elbow as he introduced himself as the nephew of the lady with the horn, whose coach he had accompanied on horseback from London.

"Fitzwilliam ma'am, Colonel of Hussars. May I offer you the support of an arm?" She thought that he could. "The shortest way to the House is the path I have just used."

"The shortest way to the Parsonage is the one I have just used. I am Charlotte Collins, the Parson's wife."

His grip on her elbow tightened and released and his look became serious.

"Mrs. Collins, I did not ride today to accompany my aunt. I heard from her about the storm and the damage it has caused. I came to assure myself of the safety of a friend, Mrs. Allen of Hutton. I found her house almost roofless, she gone to her son, and her young charge put into the care of the Parson. I am on my way just now to the Parsonage. Is what I have said true?"

"Not quite. Mrs. Allen asked my husband to restore the child to her mother. Which is what he did."

"Ah!" He regarded her closely and nodded. "Of course. I should explain to you that Major Fountain was my friend." He dismissed the matter from his mind. "Well ma'am, which arm do you prefer?"

She made her choice and they walked to the Parsonage, she wondering but not asking, why he had not consulted Mrs. Fountain.

Charlotte, limping slightly from a painful ankle, declined an offer to carry her. They knew nothing of each other, so had much to tell and separated at the Parsonage amiably well acquainted. The colonel put her into Ethel's care, and assured her that he would pay his respects when next he came.

She went gratefully to enjoy a meal and then to her chair in the little sitting room her ankle, bound in a cold wet cloth, raised on a footstool. She woke some time later as Thomas, his face creased with concern, took her hand.

"You fell?"

"Tripped. It is nothing."

"We'll hope it will be better tomorrow, then I can take you to Lady Catherine."

"Thomas, I am not a parcel. I shall visit Lady Catherine when she invites me."

He laughed.

"I cannot wait for you to meet our patroness."

Charlotte recalled the indelicate finger of her mother. 'She is not *your* patroness.'

"You are afraid she will not like me," she said playfully, then realized this was probably true though he denied it. "If Lady Catherine does not like me ....you must tell her to send me back home to my parents at Lucas Lodge. Then we can all go back to how we were before we met."

His face was either a study of uncertainty tinged with amusement or amusement tinged with uncertainty. She closed her eyes and lay back smiling. Bemused, she thought, probably summed it up. She was learning his facial expressions and this one was new. She liked it.

Lady Catherine, fatigued from her journey had retired to her apartments. Charlotte was given this information by Ethel who had so enjoyed foraging information for Molly yesterday, that she was reluctant to cease. Charlotte passed it on to her husband who went to his study to polish his sermon. She took up some silks her mother had left for her. As her hands moved carefully her mind was free to consider the extraordinary situation of Mary Fountain.

She knew that only her mother's presence yesterday had prevented her offering herself as a substitute for Mrs. Allen, she also knew that it would have been reckless, and recklessness had never been a trait of Charlotte Lucas. She did wonder, however, about Charlotte Collins. Love and marriage had changed her, but it seemed not to have strengthened her, it had weakened her and she had suffered sorely on two occasions from punishing licks of the black cat. Her wonderful good fortune had made her proud and over-confident. Charlotte Lucas would have been appalled at the behaviour of Charlotte Collins who had scourged the innocent Dorcas and risked the embarrassment of her husband. She must be more careful, especially of Rosings. She wished she need never go there again but since she knew that was impossible, she determined never to go alone.

CHAPTER

16

On Sunday evening they sat before the embers of a dying fire in their little sitting room. Thomas, long legs stretched out, seemed relaxed in sleep though his head disputed this with an occasional jerk. She ought to rouse him to go to bed but she could not bear that this special day should end. The soft silk of her dove grey wedding dress, which Thomas had not recognized, seemed a secret blessing to her fingers as they rested on her knee.

She had attended his church twice, arriving on the Parson's arm to take her seat in the Parson's rather grand family pew. Her first prayer as she put her knee on the parson's wife's hassock was to implore God to preserve the church, that day, from the presence of Lady Catherine de Bourgh and God had proved merciful. Before Matins she entertained herself and her wedding clothes by reading the Form of Solemnization of Matrimony from her Book of Common Prayer until the Reverend William Thomas Aston Collins, in cassock surplice and bands, stood before the congregation and invited it to an act of worship. Rising with the rest of the congregation but shorter than most of it, she resigned herself to being an object of curiosity until interest should wain. Released by Thomas from her pew after the Blessing, she had moved on his arm past curious parishioners to the church door where all flowed past with smiles and good wishes leaving her, inexplicably, with a warm duck egg in the palm of her left hand. She was enchanted.

Her prayers in the evening were for the sermon, which he had never mentioned but had prepared with much care. He was calm but Charlotte in her anxiety could not relax. When he climbed into the pulpit she thought he looked at her. She straightened her back, lifted her head as high as she could and looked back at him. Hands, clasped nervously on her lap, relaxed, as his clear fluent words engaged her interest in the silent church. He concluded with the tale of a storm. A storm with the awesome power to pluck a cedar like a daffodil, swoop and pounce over the parish then make a mighty swaggering departure. A bully of a storm, a drunken bully of a storm but subject always to a more awesome power that commanded it to depart without injuring a single man, woman, child or beast in the whole of the parish. Except for Sidesman Pounder, who had accidentally sat on his pipe. She felt proud of him, wished her mother could have stayed.

When he collected her from the pew, her relieved contented smile prompted responding smiles and more good wishes, and she seemed to walk back to the Parsonage in a daze.

When he expressed concern about Lady Catherine she astonished herself by warm-heartedly suggesting he should walk to Rosings before supper and inquire after her, which he did. He returned with the news from Mrs. Fountain that Lottie and her new nursemaid, Dorcas, had been invited to stay with Mrs. Allen and her son until they could all return to the house in Hutton.

As the ashes settled she savoured the day, delving within herself to find an elusive thing that was more active than contentment, for the day had been so deeply, deeply pleasing. She had come to a place where she felt she would be happy to spend the rest of her life and whatever may happen in future, on this special day she had been embraced with charity.

Charlotte had most of Monday to allow her mind to dwell happily on having been enfolded as one of Thomas's parishioners. Thomas returned in the late afternoon via Rosings. He was delighted to let her know that Lady Catherine had fully recovered and was hoping that Charlotte would accompany Thomas to take tea the following day. She decided it must have been the change in her facial expression that led him to assure her that she need not be one wit nervous about her reception. She wondered, innocently, 'if Lady Catherine had seemed nervous about receiving *her*?' It sped across his face, disbelief, a loss for words, the ghost of a smile, the bemused expression. She looked quickly away and busied herself.

On Tuesday morning Charlotte tried to describe, in a letter to her mother and father, how wonderful had been her introduction to the church of St. Andrew at Hunsford. She paused for the mid-day meal, which she ate alone, then returned to her letter until it was time to dress carefully for the short walk to Rosings. She took Thomas's arm confidently, disguising any fear that she might do or say anything that could reveal her first two visits to Rosings.

The marble bench that had witnessed her humiliating and unnecessary breakdown had disappeared, a victim of the great falling tree. They did not enter through the great front door but through the side door. Thomas was evidently one of those who came and went regularly. They passed the door of the room that she knew from her previous visits and ended up in the great marbled hall where she had stood so recently, in coat and bonnet, awaiting the opening of the doors. Thomas greeted a footman, by name, and they were taken to Lady Catherine.

Thomas had told Charlotte that they would be received in the small drawing room which was very large. It was indeed large. An island had been contrived in the middle of it with a carpet on which were sofas, tables and chairs, sufficient to accommodate a dozen persons. At present it accommodated only three. In the largest chair sat the largest person and Charlotte had no difficulty in identifying Lady Catherine but felt a momentary surprise at her elegance and near-beauty before recognizing, with her London tuned eye, the fortunate employer of an excellent lady's maid. In that moment of perception she kept her head and when Lady Catherine, giving her a smiling welcome extended a hand, she held the fingers for a count of three and gave her a smiling response. A chair was offered and as Thomas led her to it, pressing her hand she returned the pressure and continued to smile. The two other ladies present were Lady Catherine's daughter Miss de Bourgh, who offered a nervous smile and subdued murmur, and Mrs. Jenkinson her companion, who offered a genuine smile and a greeting.

Lady Catherine concentrated her attention on Charlotte.

"You have settled into your new home Mrs. Collins?

"Yes indeed, Lady Catherine. Very comfortably."

"And what is your opinion of the Parsonage."

"I consider it to be a little palace."

"You find it small?"

"I find it perfect."

Lady Catherine allowed herself a delighted laugh and invited Mrs. Jenkinson to share it.

"Perfect. You hear that Mrs. Jenkinson? We cannot improve on perfect, can we?"

"No indeed Lady Catherine. One cannot improve on perfect."

"And you are taking another servant, I understand."

Charlotte agreed that that was so and smiled. Lady Catherine waited for a moment and turned her gaze on Thomas.

"Another groom, Mr. Collins?"

"Mr. Collins is all consideration." Charlotte spoke before he could answer. "When Lady Lucas pointed out that a parson's wife might need to travel further distances than her legs can take her and might require the gig, he at once suggested a second horse and a stable lad."

Lady Catherine's attention was back on Charlotte.

"And what did your mother think of the Parsonage?"

"Lady Lucas was of the opinion that it had been refurbished and extended with great skill, and decorated and furnished with very good taste and no little expense."

Lady Catherine beamed her good opinion of Charlotte's mother.

"She should have stayed longer." She raised an admonishing finger and appealed to Mrs. Jenkinson. "We could have introduced her to Rosings."

"Sir William had imminent engagements in the City. His wife accompanies him on these occasions for there is much to see, and the evenings seem always to provide a banquet or a play or a reception at St. James's."

Lady Catherine looked slightly wistful and Charlotte, confident that she had exaggerated the gentility and sophistication of the Lucas's enough, spoke only when addressed lest a careless word should betray any suggestion of her previous visits.

The tea was brought, the footman was dismissed and Charlotte watched a ritual that was clearly performed regularly to the great enjoyment of all concerned. Thomas took upon himself the duty of serving tea, replenishing tea, urging this little savoury, that little sweetmeat on a lively party of non-resisting ladies. Affection, conversation and good humour flowed through the little group.

This tea-party was a reunion. Their last meeting was before his marriage and before Lady Catherine went on her visits. Charlotte was very surprised to learn that Miss de Bourgh and Mrs. Jenkinson had not accompanied Lady Catherine and felt a deep sense of unease that they were actually under the same roof, while she was being pummelled by the black cat. Both of them had heard the great tree fall and Lady Catherine, though she mourned its passing, was disappointed not to have been at home when it happened; the garden bench that had suffered had been fashioned from the very best Italian marble. Charlotte waited for Thomas to mention their own presence in the house that evening. He refrained, and though she knew he would not raise the subject of Lottie, she waited for someone else to do it. No one did. The entrance of a servant to remove the tea things brought a cooling to the proceedings and they said their thanks and farewells to a little group almost as sober as the one they had found.

She took his arm for the walk back. He was filled with good humour, Charlotte was filled with relief. She paused suddenly in her step. Brought thus from his own thoughts he looked down at her and when she did not speak, he did.

"I see no reason to send you back to Lucas Lodge."

"Why did you not tell her we were here on the night of the storm?"

"To what end?" It seemed a good enough response.

"Nobody mentioned Lottie."

"Nobody knew about her."

Charlotte turned and stood looking back at the house. Windows uncountable, it was immense. Lady Catherine could not possibly be aware of all that went on, a dozen Mollys would not suffice. Little Mrs. Collins, tucked away in the Parsonage, was the smallest of mice. She gave Thomas's arm an affectionate squeeze and they continued their walk home to the Parsonage in silence.

CHAPTER 18

The freedom of the gig brought a happy bloom to the life of the wife of the Parson of Hunsford. Her natural reticence as an unmarried daughter gave way to a modest self-confidence in her new status. With the encouragement of Thomas she fulfilled what she considered to be a duty to make herself known to the parish. The duty became a pleasure. Over succeeding weeks she gradually visited the hamlets of Howden, Hutton, Bellis and Culsmere. These were unsophisticated hamlets. She recognized, once again, the wisdom of Mrs. Fountain as she realized that the names on her list were those of the parish matriarchs through whom, in time, she met the mothers and families. Since she was found to be harmless, unjudging and useful she was, in time, welcomed even in times of crisis. A tumbled child needed to be set upright and have its knees rubbed. An overwrought mother required separation from a fractious baby. A cooking pot about to boil over needed a slight shift, or a pot grown sluggish for want of a stir needed a little liquid and gentle turnover. On one occasion there was the slow feeding of a frail and helpless elder who fixed his eyes on her face as she smiled and nodded and encouraged each tiny mouthful. She had gone back to the Parsonage to ask Thomas where in the Cherubim or Seraphim he could identify the Angel of Usefulness and he confessed he did not know. She thought affectionately of her mother in Meryton and London, where a printed card could bestow consequence, and was deeply grateful for her mother's true heritage of a sensible word and a useful pair of hands.

She learned much from the natives and shared it with Thomas. What she did not share was her conclusion that Lady Catherine was not much liked in the district. The building of Rosings had required the demolition of an older house, home for generations to the local squires, the last of whom now lived in Culsmere in a dower house. He was Sir James Ayres and he was currently away from home. She had assumed him literate and left a card. The general animosity had been to Sir Lewis de Bourgh, Lady Catherine's late husband, a short man whose combative personality had done little to endear him to the native dwellers. On his death Lady Catherine, grand and remote, had inherited the ill will. Social contacts of a minor nature with village and hamlets, which had started well, had largely ceased before his death some years ago.

Charlotte was loyal to her mother's prejudice against the Presumption of Lady Catherine, but felt a slight sympathy for her situation. She was relieved to discover that she saw nothing of her except, when she was present in church, an acknowledgement and a word from the very grand House Pew to the quite grand parson's pew. Rosings was a busy place when Lady Catherine was in residence. Imposing carriages went up the drive, preceded, accompanied or followed by what Thomas described as baggage wagons, and then went down the drive some days later. Thomas was always aware of who the visitors were, and with what success the visit was proceeding. As a gleaner of information he equalled Molly on these occasions but when Charlotte questioned him on the necessity of his visits to Rosings he told her, with hurt surprise, that everyone who worked there was a parishioner with a home in the surrounding hamlets. She gratefully recognized this truth, now made obvious, and was more than happy to adjust her view that adoration of Lady Catherine was the only thing that took him there. She welcomed all Lady Catherine's visitors without even setting eyes on them because when they were at Rosings, she was in no danger of having to dine there herself. She had understood from Thomas that this was a special treat in store.

Her acquaintance with those involved with the church expanded greatly over Advent, and during the final preparation of the church for Christmas, she was greeted with familiarity by several families from all the local hamlets. Some of them shared the Parson's pew with her as the church filled to over-flowing for the wonderful, music filled, Christmas services. After Christmas it snowed and since the Family was visiting relations, the lane to Rosings showed only horse and foot prints as not a single carriage entered or left. Charlotte was filled with love, peace and contentment.

After the turn of the year the family returned to Rosings, and when they had had time to settle down, the Parson and his wife were invited to dine. These occasions were precious to Thomas and he showed his appreciation so openly that it was sufficient that Charlotte should simply smile on the company of Lady Catherine, Miss de Bourgh and Mrs. Jenkinson. Her visits to London with her parents before her marriage had required one or two rather grand garments, and these she wore in rotation as the occasion demanded, and they proved suitably modest compared with those of Lady Catherine. By her third dinner at Rosings, Charlotte, who had observed that in huge rooms, the space beyond the assembled company seemed to shrink away, ceased to be awed by size. She maintained a pleasant expression, and spoke only when required, which was slightly more often than Miss de Bourgh. Conversation at dinner was dominated by Lady Catherine who had very strong opinions, when those opinions were challenged by Thomas or Mrs. Jenkinson, Charlotte was attentive and grateful. As she was always seeking traits of character in Lady Catherine that would explain Thomas's devotion, and never finding them, she was disappointed. The dinners were always excellent but so were dinners at the Parsonage, and it was to these they returned when the visiting season re-commenced.

19

The preparation, towards Spring, for a visit of her father her sister and Lizzie Bennet proved a real pleasure for Charlotte and was accomplished without fuss. Sir William had tried to persuade his wife to join the party but she had remained firm and Charlotte was certain that she had not even told him of the evening when, overtaken by events, she had been abducted into Rosings.

The delicacy of the situation between Thomas and Lizzie perplexed Charlotte somewhat before the visit. Lizzie was her friend and, importantly, Thomas's remote cousin. There may be some residual embarrassment between them but she was certain there were no emotional regrets and contact between Thomas and his only relations was of prime importance. It could not be sacrificed, either to an unfortunate proposal of marriage, or the existence of an entail. She simply reminded him that they were coming and gave him the dates. He said it should be interesting.

The day before their arrival Thomas had hoped aloud that since Lady Catherine had no visitors at present she would offer their guests hospitality. Charlotte hazarded a guess that since Lady Catherine sought mild excitement by having the Parson and his wife to dinner, she would be unable to resist the temptation of new faces. She was nurturing his bemused expression and when it appeared with a reproachful shake of the head she laughed aloud. When they were invited she simply remarked that dinners at Rosings were always excellent.

Lady Catherine was in high good humour, charmingly elegant and quite blooming, courtesy of Alice her maid, whom Charlotte hoped to meet some day. Her Ladyship obviously relished the company of men and to the observing Charlotte, charmed Sir William who was flattered and instantly won over. Meanwhile Thomas, telling them of Rosings and its park, said everything Lady Catherine could have wished to say herself. Charlotte, Elizabeth, Maria, Miss de Bourgh and Mrs. Jenkinson were chiefly spectators of the performance at the dinner table their reward being the excellent meal before them. Charlotte, on the same side of the table as Elizabeth could not see her but half hoped for, half dreaded, a demonstration of the wit and wildness that both relieved and flawed the Bennet family.

When the ladies withdrew from the dining room Lady Catherine settled herself comfortably in her chair on the carpet in the small drawing room and beaming with good humour set herself to satisfy her curiosity about the lives of others. Maria, terrified throughout the whole evening was mute, so Lady Catherine set herself to catechize Elizabeth about her home, her parents, her sisters, their status, their social life, their prospects and their shortcomings. Charlotte, powerless to intervene, sat through a demonstration of gross ill manners that appalled her. Lady Catherine was without shame or restraint and Charlotte winced at the indignity to which she had exposed her friend, admiring all the while Elizabeth's resilience and restraint.

She was out of patience with her husband and her father, neither of whom had witnessed the catechizing, but both of whom considered the evening a great success. When Elizabeth retired, Charlotte followed her to her room to apologize.

"I would rather not have invited you at all than expose you to that, but you had the best of it, Lizzie. Her gross bluntness was exposed by your good humoured fencing. You punctured her certainty and I call that a victory for you." Elizabeth smiled at her friend.

"We wondered, did we not, how you would cope with Lady Catherine?"

"I smile, concealing resentful tolerance when I am unable to avoid her." Elizabeth gasped at such candour. "Thomas's affection for her is sincere. Some day I hope to discover why because I cannot see that she deserves it. The House entertained very little over January and February and we dined there twice a week, clearly to relieve the tedium of the three ladies having to dine alone every day. The dinners are always excellent and it satisfies something deep in Thomas to carve at Lady Catherine's table but you are not obliged to go and I will make your excuses if you wish."

Elizabeth, reasoning that Lady Catherine having roasted her once was unlikely to do so again, saw no necessity to deprive herself of any entertainment on offer. The subsequent arrival of Lady Catherine's nephews, Mr. Darcy and Colonel Fitzwilliam, provided her with an opportunity to demonstrate her considerable social skills. Charlotte had some sympathy for the reserved Mr. Darcy who was quite put in the shade by the easy intercourse of his cousin. Her greatest pleasure however was to observe how the artifice of the incomparable Alice and the assumed gaiety of Lady Catherine, melted away before the natural grace and engaging good humour of her friend Lizzie.

Colonel Fitzwilliam paid his respects to Mrs. Collins at the Parsonage daily, sometimes accompanied by Mr. Darcy. Neither the colonel nor Charlotte referred to their previous meeting, but their companionship was easy and the visits, though brief, were pleasant for everyone and delighted Thomas though he was rarely present. Charlotte expressed her conviction to both Elizabeth and Thomas that a breathing space in the Parsonage was a valuable release from a whole day spent at Rosings.

Finally, she concluded that Colonel Fitzwilliam had not approached Mrs. Fountain about the whereabouts of Lottie after the storm, because such an association of visitor and servant would have risked the kind of embarrassment that Mrs. Fountain had warned her to avoid.

CHAPTER

20

Charlotte walked the path at the edge of the estate. She had taken possession of it, always expecting and always finding solitude. She wore a light coat, for sitting in half shade, but no hat because the air was warm. The trees, she had discovered that they were elms, were now in full green leaf and whispering with the breeze. She greeted the tree that had broken her fall, on the day she had met the Colonel, and carried on to the end of the path where a comfortable garden bench in dappled sunlight waited for her. Behind the bench was a tall mixed hedge that marked another boundary. She sat and closed her eyes to accustom herself to the silence that was a myriad small sounds then opened them to absorb the stillness of a myriad small movements. It was pleasant but she had not come for pleasure. She had come to think.

Thomas had shaken her awake in the early morning to rescue her from a distressing dream. Because he had woken her in the course of it she remembered it clearly. She had been fighting her way through a huge spider's web seeking Thomas to rescue him before the great spider could consume him. In her distress she had almost told him the dream but fortunately her waking wits had lied on her behalf and said she could not remember.

She sat on the bench and asked herself if she really thought that Lady Catherine would eat Thomas. No, she did not, but it was the web that intrigued her. If Lady Catherine was the spider the web must be Rosings. The dream had revealed a truth about her relationship with the house. She sighed. Rosings had not been kind to her, had not welcomed her. She shook herself impatiently. That was nonsense! Buildings do not have emotions. If she had walked up to Rosings and beaten her head against its bricks it would not have felt pity or even puzzlement.

Her two unfortunate experiences, now some time past, had simply reinforced a prejudice, caught from her mother, at Lady Catherine's presumption. But *had* Lady Catherine been presumptuous? If Thomas had brought news of his forthcoming marriage in the expectation of it taking place in his church at Hunstan, Lady Catherine had responded with an act of generosity.

So, was Lady Catherine presumptuous? She smiled, trying to imagine Thomas's face if she asked him that question. He loved Rosings, he blossomed there in conversation with Lady Catherine and Mrs. Jenkinson while Anne de Bourgh rarely spoke and Charlotte limited herself to responses. Charlotte went to Rosings carefully disguising from Thomas her reluctance to do so but feared she could never be herself as the guest of Lady Catherine de Bourgh. She reminded herself that one great advantage of that, was the pleasure with which she always returned to the person-sized comforts of the Parsonage.

She patted the wooden arm affectionately and reminded herself that benches do not have emotions either. She had sat here often and thought of Mary Fountain, a secret invisible presence at the heart of Rosings. Thomas saw her frequently and when Charlotte asked him to pass on her good wishes, he did so and reported that she smiled and thanked him, but she never reciprocated with a similar request.

Charlotte had not been aware of Mrs. Allen until the dramas of the storm, but she had sought out the house in Hutton and followed the stages of its repair. When the repair was complete she had visited, offered her card and been welcomed by Mrs. Allen. They had developed a liking for each other. She presumed that Mrs. Fountain had left her off the visiting list because of Lottie, but she saw no reason to avoid the house now on that account. Mrs. Allen must have told Mrs. Fountain that Lottie and Charlotte had become friends. She could not imagine the hardship of a mother thus separated from a child. She sighed and rose. She needed cheering up. Thomas would do that, it must be about time for his return from a Rosings tea-party. He would be bursting with bonhomie.

Thomas was already at home and solemn faced. He fetched her from the door as she entered the Parsonage, still in her in coat, and led her into the little sitting room and then to a chair.

"Grave news Charlotte," he warned her, unnecessarily, when she was seated. "Lady Catherine's nephew has drowned while taking a tour of the Picturesque on the River Wye." Charlotte's heart turned over for Mr. Darcy and Colonel Fitzwilliam as she wondered which one he meant. "Colonel Fitzwilliam has gone to recover his brother's body." He paused, then spoke with awe. "The Colonel is now heir to the Earldom."

Charlotte who seemed not to have breathed since she entered the house, inhaled deeply. She acknowledged, with some surprise, her deep affection for Mr. Darcy and the Colonel and was overjoyed for them. Her regret at the death of someone she did not know was subsumed in the shock that someone she did know was the sister and daughter of an Earl. She wondered whether her question about Lady Catherine's presumption was still a proper question. She decided that it ought to be but probably was not.

Having imparted the dreadful news, Thomas was able to relax. Charlotte gave her coat to Ethel and Thomas asked for a pot of tea. Over a cup, he told her that the tea party had been drawing to a close when Lady Catherine was told that there was a messenger from her brother. She had left the small drawing room in surprise, and was absent for some time before returning with a very high colour and holding a letter. Thomas thought she had seemed more angry than grief-stricken as she quite brutally announced the death of her nephew, at which Miss de Bourgh had collapsed in a dead faint. Thomas, seeing no role for himself in the succeeding upheaval, paused only to express condolence to Lady Catherine and came home. Charlotte did not bother to ask Thomas why he had not told her that Lady Catherine was sister to an Earl, he would simply express surprise that she had not known it already.

Rosings went into mourning. Thomas clearly felt the occurrence so personally that Charlotte asked him if he wished the Parsonage to go into mourning. He embraced her warmly for her sensitivity but said that since the young man was neither friend nor relation such an act was not necessary. Entertaining at Rosings ceased. Perversely, once the dining room at Rosings was no longer open to her, Charlotte was nostalgic and Thomas clearly disappointed. Charlotte introduced Mrs.Wilby to her mother's book of collected recipes, and on two evenings, which would have been Rosing's evenings, Mrs. Wilby cooked 'Lady Lucas' consolation dinners. This amused Thomas who was suitably impressed and entertained.

According to Ethel, the usually reliable informant, mourning at Rosings consisted chiefly in the footmen donning dark livery, kept over since the death of Sir Lewis de Bourgh. Everyone had walked on tiptoe and whispered for the first couple of days then forgot to do so except when in the presence of the family. One imminent visit of a friend of Lady Catherine had been cancelled. The need to do this had displeased her a good deal and she had not concealed her displeasure.

Since Thomas provided most interest and amusement at the dining table, Charlotte found herself wondering just how long Lady Catherine could spare him.

CHAPTER

21

Lady Catherine, piqued that she had been given notice of the tragic event but no explanation of how or why it had happened, sent back with her brother's messenger a request for more detail. Her request had been ignored. She had experienced more than one tour of the Picturesque on the River Wye. They had been peaceful, even stately. Learning nothing further from her brother and unable to reconcile such peaceful rural progress with a fatality, she sought further information privately from friends in London and the country. She was aware that her nephew kept the same kind of company as his wilful father, and she had never been sure whether she was totally abhorrent or thrillingly proud of her brother who, when challenged to a duel, had fired a fatal shot. She suspected a duel and meant to know.

Charlotte (who had discovered that Lady Catherine could only spare Thomas for eight days) was in the small drawing with Thomas, Miss de Bourgh and Mrs. Jenkinson. Their black dresses confirmed the mourning but the sincere welcoming greetings and smiles of the two ladies heartened Charlotte. They were awaiting Lady Catherine who had been delayed by a messenger from the Earl. They were aware that the funeral would take place at Gavelston but the date was as yet uncertain. The wait was a long one, conversation flowed easily and Charlotte was completely relaxed.

Lady Catherine arrived with the impact of a whirlwind. Magnificently dressed in green, with a face like a pink wound, her voice preceded her as she entered the great room while the footmen cowered at the door.

"He has forbidden me Gavelston! Forbidden me to enter my own home! Forbidden me the funeral! He has accused me of generating slander! Admonished friends of a lifetime for encouraging me to bring the family into disrepute..." She flung herself into her great chair and Charlotte, cowering backwards, felt the others do the same, away from the heat of her anger. "Me! He accuses me! I have spent a lifetime defending his reputation against slander, and also that of his son. He forbids me, accuses me, strikes at my friends and the reason must be that I was *right*. There *must* have been a duel. Nothing else will answer. Let him cut himself off from me, if he wishes, and cut off his son also. There will be no further mourning in this house. It is his retribution!" The terrible word hung in the air. Frozen with shock no-one moved as she spat the word again into the air. "Retribution." Charlotte gazed in horror as Thomas rose and stood in front of Lady Catherine.

"No Lady Catherine!" His voice was loud. Everybody sat upright. Startled, Lady Catherine was still for a moment, then lifted her hands to push him away but he took hold of them, and they wrestled horribly for control as she stared at him in astonishment and he spoke loudly back into her face. "No! No! No! A young man is dead. His soul is in peril! We must mourn and grieve until he is safe. You have your own chapel. I will discover the time and we shall have a service for him here at Rosings." He released her hands. "And put retribution from your mind. Do not invent a duel. The young man died of drowning." He excused them and they left while Lady Catherine's mouth was still open.

Charlotte woke next morning with Thomas warm beside her. They had walked home, in silence, and she had gone to bed alone, while Thomas went on to his church.

Uneasy days followed. Invitations to dine were withdrawn. Thomas planned a service. He continued his usual patterns of behaviour, including visits to parishioners at Rosings. He did not mention the incident and she could not bring herself to do so. She had a chair and a cushion taken into the potting shed, and when he went there she followed him with a book or some stitching. He smiled and shook his head, but did not speak and each continued, silently absorbed and in quiet companionship. She thought how fortunate it was that before their marriage each had been accustomed to silence, and it had become a further warm sympathetic communion.

She also, however, sought some distraction in a parish visit.

CHAPTER

22

Always welcomed at Larkspur Cottage since the return of Mrs. Allen and Lottie, Charlotte was disappointed to learn that Mrs. Allen was not at home. As she was about to get into the gig Mrs. Allen's maid came running to call her back. In a corner of the hall there stood a trunk and packages. In the drawing room Mrs. Allen and Mrs. Fountain sat like carved statues. Neither woman rose to greet her. Nor did Lottie, clinging to her mother's knee, run towards her. Charlotte's greeting died on her lips.

"What awful thing has happened?"

"You have not heard?"

"Oh Mrs. Allen, not bad news of your son?"

"No, my dear." Mrs. Allen looked towards Mrs. Fountain.

"Lady Catherine banished me today, instantly, from Rosings. She has refused to give me a reason."

Charlotte absorbed the immensity of this statement as she took a seat.

"You cannot think of any way in which you might have offended her?"

Mrs. Fountain shook her head.

"I have known Lady Catherine for almost a year but I did not recognize this woman. She was a raging tower of anger. I pleaded, tried to reason, and finally I demanded; to no avail. I do not understand why she has done this."

A shiver ran through Charlotte as she remembered Lady Catherine's anger. In Mrs. Fountain's voice, calm and low though it was, Charlotte detected despair.

"Have you decided where you will go?"

"Oh yes." There was a rueful humour in her voice, "I must ask a home of my sister's husband." She paused, looked at Charlotte as she continued. "This is a man who, despite discouragement, was my own persistent suitor and who took, and forcefully expressed, deep offence at my refusal. His indifference would be a blessing but," her voice fell, "in truth, I anticipate ill will." She paused. "And I am fearful of malice." She lifted Lottie onto her lap and wrapped protective arms about her.

The chilling words and the hopeless voice of a mother helpless to protect her child shocked Charlotte, made her shiver, she thought of their natural protector, husband and father, dead and helpless in the war, and felt an immense impotent outrage. Through the confusions of her mind she heard herself speak.

"I own a house in Meryton."

The two ladies looked at her in disbelief.

"How dare she do this? It will destroy you in the world. She must know that. It must be her intention." Both women looked at her in shock.

She could hardly believe that she had uttered those words, but was convinced they were true. The deep sympathy, gratitude and regard she felt for this woman, could not let Charlotte see her young daughter sacrificed on the altar of Lady Catherine's anger, whatever the cause.

"Does your sister expect you?"

"I have not yet written, but I must not delay. I impose on Mrs. Allen." Mrs. Allan took her hand.

"Haste must not force us into a foolish decision. What does Mrs. Collins suggest?"

Charlotte clutched at a straw.

"I do not know if the house is occupied. Six days should be long enough to ask the question and receive the answer. If it is not occupied we shall need a coach to Hertfordshire ..."

"I think I can answer for my son." Said Mrs. Allen faintly.

Charlotte could not descry a future if the house was occupied, which she admitted to herself was likely. She had been reckless beyond imagination. She returned to the parsonage, stunned by what she had done. Thomas was out of doors, overlooking the paddock.

"Did you know that Mrs. Fountain has been dismissed." He nodded.

"Have you been to Rosings?" He nodded again.

"What are they saying about it in the House?

"Nothing, hardly anybody knows yet."

"Did you see Lady Catherine?"

"Briefly. She is quite adamant, un-approachable."

"Why?"

"I do not know."

"Refusing to give a reason to Mrs. Fountain is very wicked." She looked at his troubled face, waited for a while for him to speak. "Thomas, is there anything that you and I together can do to help Mrs. Fountain?"

"No. Lady Catherine is confident she can make her home with a brother-in-law."

"What if she does not like him?"

"If he gives Lottie a home, gratitude will make her like him."

She could say nothing further. She began to walk away but curiosity brought her back.

"What will happen without a Housekeeper?"

He shook his head.

"I don't know. There is a Steward, Mr. Herbert."

"What is he like? Could he do something for Mrs. Fountain?"

"He is Lady Catherine's servant."

She dragged her leaden feet back to the Parsonage. She could not tell him what she had done but she would not abandon Lottie, whose need was great and immediate.

CHAPTER

23

Sir William and Lady Lucas returned home after a three day visit to London that had been filled with business and pleasure. They anticipated a late supper and a quick retirement. A letter from Charlotte awaited them. Sir William, fatigued from the business of the days and the entertainments of the evenings, urged his wife to delay the pleasure of opening it until the morning. Lady Lucas had it open before he had finished speaking. Leaving her travelling cloak with Molly and be-speaking supper the moment it was ready, she repaired to an armchair by the fire in the dining room. The sudden lifting of her head and straightening of her back as she began to read sent a message of alarm to her husband. He took a chair by the fire and waited.

"Dearest Mother,

I write this much disturbed. You made it clear to me that Mary Fountain could not be my friend because she was a servant. She is no longer a servant, having been dismissed *instantly and without reason*, by Lady Catherine and I claim her as a friend. She is now *homeless*. Her sole relation is a sister married to a man whom Mrs. Fountain *does not respect. He is aware of this and their dislike is mutual*. Her means are small. They have empowered her to house her child and a nursemaid with a widow in Hutton. But Mother, you know this. Her name is Lottie. *You nursed *her*, please remember! (Mother, sadly I find myself at odds with Thomas, who I know is unhappy, but puts his faith in Lady Catherine, but I put my faith in Mrs. Fountain. We married for better or for worse, and we will both of us have to remember that at a time in the future that I dare not even contemplate.) You wrote something of the change of lease at the old house in Meryton. What happened? I paid less attention to it than I ought. This woman, whom I really admire, *needs* a *home* for herself and her child. I detect that she is *particularly anxious* for Lottie I *implore you and my father to find one for her.* It would be a miracle if it could be the house in Meryton. I am so angry with Lady Catherine that I cannot speak her name, indeed I can hardly write it. She is so arrogant that she will *not even give* a *reason* to a woman whose life will be *destroyed*, she *must know* that it is an act of *utmost cruelty.*

Mother, for many years you and I have not only been Mother and Daughter, we have been Friends. I call upon your Friendship, unreservedly. Mrs. Allen hopes that her son can have his carriage at his mother's house, Larkspur Cottage, Hutton, with instructions to take Mrs. Fountain, her daughter Lottie and a nursemaid, initially to Lucas Lodge and further as requested six days beyond the date on this letter. I only wish the coach could be going from my house in defiance of the cruel woman but that cannot be.

Mrs. Fountain strains to seem calm, but I know that she is distraught for Lottie's sake. Please find it in your heart to help, and to send a sympathetic message to Mrs. Fountain at Larkspur Cottage, Hutton.

Your loving daughter and friend,
Charlotte."

"Oh Mother I do not know if I have done a terribly wrong thing. And yet I cannot do *nothing*. *Somebody* must protect this woman and her small daughter from the *raw malice* of Lady Catherine. *Somebody strong*, and so I think of *you and my father.*

I urge you to be very cautious about what is said within the hearing of anyone who might gossip in Meryton. If Mrs. Fountain arrived to find her reputation already in ruins, it would be a total triumph for Lady Catherine. I have prevailed upon Thomas for the time being to keep his cousin, Mr. Bennet, in ignorance of the affair. Oh Mother, I have read all this again and it seems such a jumble, it hardly makes sense but I am despairing and do not know how to seek a better way of asking for your help."

She handed it to her husband.
"She is in despair. It is hurriedly written and heavily underscored."
He read, serious faced.
"The house is occupied."
"Is there nowhere else? Think William think!" Sir William furrowed his weary brow. "We must find somewhere, William, or have them here."
Molly, and another maid entering with supper drew them to the table. From there he went to his bed and his wife to her writing desk.

"Dear Mrs. Fountain,
What a great pleasure it will be for me to renew acquaintance with you and your daughter, and to continue that acquaintance when you make your home among us, as you shall, very soon. You have won the high regard of Mrs. Collins, and Sir William and I prize the value of that regard. You and your daughter will be welcome in our home.

Yours sincerely,
Elizabeth Lucas"

"My Dear Charlotte,
It pains us that you should be so distraught but pleases us that you had the confidence and good sense to act as you did. Have no concerns for Mrs. Fountain and her daughter, they will be welcomed here and a home found. I have written to her with every assurance of a welcome. I

shall dispatch that letter and this one together, for delivery on the same day. When you have yours, she will have hers. You may be resisting the temptation to get on the coach with them and come home yourself. You are right to resist. We returned this evening from London thinking we were exhausted, to face your letter! Now we know we are exhausted. I go upstairs expecting to find your father snoring.

Your very good Friend and Mother."

24

Sir William was not snoring. He was awake and unnaturally querulous.

"How do we know that woman was not dishonest or disrespectful?"

"Oh William!"

"Well?"

"We trust Charlotte's judgement."

"And is Charlotte a Justice of the Peace?"

This was serious. Lady Lucas had a sense of her daughter's unease in the parsonage. It affected her now at Lucas Lodge. She brought his gown.

"Sit up William, I cannot speak to you when you are not upright."

They sat together on the side of the bed, facing Lady Lucas's dressing mirror. She took his hand.

"We must assume that she is honest."

"Why did Lady Catherine dismiss her?"

"Lady Catherine will not tell her."

"How do you know that is true?"

"I trust Charlotte's judgement." Her voice became urgent. "If she has dismissed Mrs. Fountain in this way, without telling her why, she must know it will destroy her."

"Preposterous! Why would she do such a thing? You forget I have met Lady Catherine. I have dined at her table. She is a charming, elegant, gracious lady."

"And you forget that I have met Mrs. Fountain and she really *is* a charming, gracious brave lady, the widow of a soldier and mother of a young child, both rendered homeless by Lady Catherine, without explanation. Do you think we should not help Charlotte to find her a home?"

"We should not encourage her to risk the displeasure of their patroness. She is a powerful woman."

With that, Sir William lay down and pulled up the covers. His wife clenched her teeth, then unclenched them. She could not believe what she had heard. She breathed deeply and spoke calmly.

"I have written letters to Charlotte, and to Mrs. Fountain, offering our help. Am I to destroy them?"

"Yes."

"I must instruct Charlotte that her father says she must give way to Lady Catherine's will?"

"Yes." He turned away from her onto his side. She caught sight of her face in the dressing mirror, twisted with anger and disappointment. Hot tears welled up in her eyes. She could not remember when last she had been moved to anger and tears. This was betrayal. Overwhelmed suddenly by weariness she sat quite still and stared at her unhappy image that stared implacably back. She stood up.

"Very well, William. She *is* a powerful woman. She has divided *us*. You are for her. I am for Charlotte. Forgive me, it makes me upset." She picked up her gown. "I shall sleep on the couch in your dressing room. Tomorrow morning I will destroy the letters, and write others to your dictation."

He made no response. He was asleep, but his face did not look restful, it was scowling and ugly. She spoke softly and tearfully to his sleeping face.

"Oh William! I cannot believe that you would abandon Charlotte to ingratiate yourself with that woman!" She went to the dressing room and lay on the couch but there was no sleep for her, as deeply buried unease from the past rose to accuse her.

She had been relieved that Charlotte had never resented her younger siblings; there had been many 'Little Madams' among her acquaintance whom she knew wouldn't have been so amenable; but it was she who had allowed Charlotte's sisterly affection to become mothering. Preoccupied with the many and sometimes risky commercial decisions that her husband increasingly shared with her, she had known an interest beyond infants and she had indulged it, and revelled in the new relationship with William. She had been a very happy woman, brushing from her mind the thought that the younger children should have been Charlotte's own that she, herself, should have been their grandmother. Finding a husband for the invaluable Charlotte had never been one of her pre-occupations. However, Charlotte had found one for herself, and think what one might of Thomas Collins, Charlotte was happy with her choice; happy Charlotte was risking everything she valued most, she must be given support. She resolved to try a soft persuasion of her husband in the morning when he was rested and amiable. This relaxing thought allowed fatigue to have its way and she slipped into sleep.

She woke with a start as a cold hand touched her cheek. Her husband stood beside her in his nightshirt, with a lighted candle.

"William! What are you doing?"

"What are *you* doing here?"

"I didn't want to disturb you."

"Well you have."

"Get in, you're freezing." She pulled back the bedclothes moved sideways and he climbed into the small bed.

"I went down stairs, I never thought you would be here."

"Without your gown and slippers! Did you feel unwell?"

"No. I just turned over to tell you that we should put our money on Charlotte and you'd gone.

"You think it is a wager?"

"Yes."

"Oh William! Turn on your side and I will warm your back. Lift your feet and rest them on mine. You must not put your health at risk, what would we do if you took a fever? What changed your mind?"

"It changed itself and woke me up to let me know. It does that some-times" He snuffed the candle and snuggled back.

"Oh William!"

He yawned deeply and went quickly to sleep. His devoted, relieved, thankful and slightly bemused wife took rather longer.

25

Lady Lucas, once engaged, had managed the removal of Mrs. Fountain to a new home. Charlotte, relieved, but enmeshed in guilt and deception had no idea how to confess to Thomas what she had done. Furthermore, once her own anxiety was relieved she noticed that Thomas, himself, seemed uncertain and anxious. As they knelt at their prie dieux her evening prayers had finished before his and her opened eyes looked onto his bowed head. The Third Collect was no longer enough. She had known that providing the Service he had promised was causing him difficulty, a service for the Burial of the Dead required a body. He raised his head and she smiled, sympathetically, into the blue eyes.

"Whatever you do will be excellent and appropriate." Her confidence was absolute.

"The Earl has relaxed his prohibition on Lady Catherine's attendance at the funeral at Gavelston."

"And...?"

"She thinks he should apologize first." He laughed and shook his head. "I shall hold a Service whether she is here or not, others have expressed an interest, but I fear I have allowed my concern for her to overlay my duty to the young man. It is a lapse I must discuss with the Dean." This was no time to burden him with her own transgression, it must wait until the Service was over.

Charlotte slept soundly and rose to face the day in a confident state of mind that prevailed until early afternoon when the delivery of another letter from her mother set her pulse racing. Lady Lucas was not a woman of extravagant habits and Charlotte was not optimistic about any message it might contain. The news was shocking. Never had the transparency of the Bennet household to the scrutiny of the outside world, yielded the town of Meryton a more delicious morsel. Lydia Bennet had eloped with a soldier. She dropped the letter as if it had burned her and cringed back, pressed hands over her eyes and grieved for Lizzie and Jane, their lives blighted forever by a stupid reckless spoilt child. Wicked, wicked, Lydia! The wave of anger passed leaving her deeply sad. She wanted to write immediately to Lizzie and Jane telling them that she was their friend forever, and that beside her there would always be a place for them, but she knew she could not do that now. The practical part of her noted that while the disgraced Lydia occupied the gossips of Meryton, the disgraced Mrs. Fountain might slip into their midst without remark. She was obliged to pass on the dreadful news to her husband. She hoped it might give him some respite from the unnatural obsession he had developed with the difficulties of providing a service that would satisfy Lady Catherine. It galvanized him into writing a letter, and the distraction absorbed him so deeply that he failed to notice the departure of Lady Catherine's coach as it passed the Parsonage. He would be disappointed, they had been invited to dine with Lady Catherine for the first time since the eruption. What a dilemma! Should they just go? Or just not go? Either could be equally embarrassing!

Ethel, bringing a letter for Charlotte some time later, told her that Lady Catherine was bound for the funeral at Gavelston. It had been a sudden decision. The coach house was still bristling and the kitchen was still preparing this evening's dinner, to which Mr. Collins and his wife were expected, for a dining room that was only used when Lady Catherine was in residence. Charlotte put these two irritations down to the absence of a Housekeeper and was pleased.

The letter explained that Lady Catherine was no longer in residence at Rosings but that the Parson and his wife were still expected to dine, and the writer looked forward to welcoming them to Rosings. The letter was from Anne de Bourgh.

For dinner with Miss de Bourgh they foregathered in the drawing room that Charlotte knew from her first two visits. She looked round it with pleased recognition and also noticed that Miss de Bourgh looked taller and was without the numerous scarves and wraps that usually encumbered her. They dined in the room adjacent. The time passed quickly with the easy informal companionship that Charlotte had so admired at the tea party, but without the constraint of Lady Catherine. Though Miss de Bourgh, preoccupied, took little part in conversation, Charlotte joined in with ease and pleasure. They learned from Mrs. Jenkinson that she had been a school-mate of Lady Catherine at a boarding school in Scarborough. She had stayed on at the school as a teacher. She had married a subsequent proprietor and inherited the school when he died in a riding accident. When Lady Catherine visited her old school seeking a governess for her young daughter, the friends met again. She sold the school and moved to Rosings.

They were offered a carriage ride to the Parsonage after dinner, as was usual, but decided to walk and left Rosings by the side entrance. Charlotte felt completely at ease. It was the first enjoyable evening she had spent at Rosings. Her mind had much to turn over. She felt, gratefully, that she had been welcomed into the friendship of the other three. It had not been a sad evening considering the imminent funeral, quite the opposite, but Charlotte had become gently aware that if there was any genuine place of mourning at Rosings, it was most likely to be in the apartments of Anne de Bourgh. Feeling some distraction might be welcomed she had mention Parish visits the next day and wondered if the ladies would care to join her. Mrs. Jenkinson had declined but Anne had accepted eagerly. Charlotte felt compelled to warn her that these were not normal social visits but Miss de Bourgh had responded by asking at what time she should present herself at the Parsonage?

26

Charlotte revised her assumption that the presence of Miss de Bourgh would please those who normally welcomed her own visits. The unease and brevity of the first visit two led her, in some embarrassment, to make for the home of Mrs. Allen. This visit proved more exciting than Charlotte expected, and it was the silent Miss de Bourgh who proved most vocal. She remembered that the parson had been called to a lady of that name in the early hours of the morning after the great storm, to administer the last rites, and expressed astonishment at her wonderful recovery. Mrs. Allen told her the truth about that emergency summons for the parson.

"Goodness! Mrs. Fountain had a daughter?"

Mrs. Allen explained how Major Fountain had died before Lottie was born.

"Poor Mrs. Fountain." Miss de Bourgh was moved. "I really liked her, why did she leave us?"

Mrs. Allen did not hesitate.

"Lady Catherine dismissed her."

"Really? Why did she do that?"

"She would not say."

"Mrs. Fountain would not tell you?"

"Lady Catherine would not tell Mrs. Fountain."

Miss de Bourgh was shocked. Mrs. Allen took her hand.

"My dear do not be sad. No one else is. The change brought nothing but happiness for Mrs. Fountain and Lottie. I am her friend and correspond with her, if you wish I will remember you to her and express your regret at her departure."

Mrs. Allen expressed surprise that Miss de Bourgh was abroad, since it was widely understood in the neighbourhood that she was of a delicate constitution. Anne de Bourgh shared with them three years of her life when she had, indeed, been an invalid. When she slowly succumbed to, and then slowly recovered from, a mysterious wasting disease. She attributed her survival to Mrs. Jenkinson who had fought off all physicians who recommended leeching. She had become her nurse, and had been ready at all times to tend to her, or to relieve her tedium with a tale of epic or romance. Despite constant demand, her resources had never failed. Detecting some scepticism in Mrs. Allen, Miss de Bourgh with insistence mentioned stories from the Old Testament, the Classical myths, the Round Table of King Arthur and the Legends of Charlemagne until Mrs. Allen raised her hands with a laugh and a gesture of submission, but Miss de Bourgh had not done. During the long recuperation Mrs. Jenkinson had instructed her in drawing and painting and they had illustrated several of those stories. Perhaps they would do her the favour of coming to Rosings to see them? This spontaneous invitation took Charlotte and Mrs. Allen by surprise. Mrs. Allen, recovering first, thanked Miss de Bourgh with evident pleasure for her kind invitation and said she hardly went abroad, but would give it serious consideration. Charlotte related all this to Thomas on her return. He suggested that since news of Miss de Bourgh's presence must be spreading rapidly around the parish, not to take her next time might cause widespread disappointment.

Charlotte, always an interested observer of others had wondered from the beginning whether there might be a similar trait in the unnaturally silent Miss Anne de Bourgh. She had detected no evidence of it until a dinner at Rosings when she had allowed her gaze to slip away from

Lady Catherine and met the speculative glance of Miss de Bourgh upon her. The eye contact had embarrassed both of them and been instantly broken, but it had excited Charlotte. It had also alarmed her. She dared not risk a trespass that might set loose the chastising tongue of the black cat, but the events following the sudden departure of Lady Catherine had transformed Charlotte's relationship with Mrs. Jenkinson and Miss de Bourgh, and she was grateful.

As she knelt that evening at her prie-dieu Charlotte felt, as she often did, a deep sense of gratitude to Mr. Beevers for his strange but wonderful gift. When she opened her eyes Thomas's look was already upon her. He was at ease with himself in spite of his 'lapse'. He had reverted to the Third Collect. It seemed an opportune moment to ask if he intended to keep his mother in a box forever. He closed his eyes and his brow furrowed. It seemed a long silence to Charlotte as she waited. His answer came eventually. No, he did not.

27

He put the box into her hands next day before he set off for his ride to the Deanery. It was pale unpolished wood, soiled and weathered with handling; one person only from boyhood to manhood. She considered the effort it must have taken to share it. She fetched her tape and measured it, eight inches by six inches, quite small, but not perhaps to a young boy warned to keep it close. She sat and nursed it for a minute thinking of Thomas's struggle to give her a 'yes', then she opened it quickly and the serene young face with its suggestion of a smile made her smile in response. This little person had spent too long concealed and drenched in sadness, she must be free to see and be seen. She was pondering where to hang it when Ethel surprised her with a visitor's card. Sir James Ayres was returning her call.

Sir James was the first, and only, person on whom she had left her card. She received him willingly and he was instantly at ease. She saw a smart robust young man of middle height, his dark locks overdue for shearing and his complexion tinted by open air pursuits. He refused refreshment since his visit could only be brief, but remained for almost an hour. Charlotte surmised that his call had been generated by a visit to Mrs. Allen, whom he claimed as an acquaintance of old. His wish was to convey to herself and Mr. Collins his admiration for their generosity of spirit towards Mrs. Fountain. Discomfited by the thought that Thomas might discover her deception from someone other than herself, she resolved to confess the moment he returned.

Other conversation flowed easily. He inquired very kindly after Miss de Bourgh and was surprised to learn from Charlotte that she had not accompanied her mother to Gavelston. He had known and liked her when they were children, and relationships had been amiable. Was she then not to attend Grendon's funeral? He explained to Charlotte, that the heir to the Earldom was Lord Grendon, a young man he had known from childhood. They had last associated in Venice and Ravenna, in the days before Napoleon. The tragic accident had shocked him deeply. Was Miss de Bourgh, he wondered, not well enough to travel? Charlotte could not admit to knowing anything of Miss de Bourgh's health.

"To miss her cousin's service in the Gavelston chapel will be an added sorrow for her."

"Mr. Collins is conducting a service in the chapel at Rosings." This last information interested him. He begged her to pass his respects to Mr. Collins and departed.

She had entertained him in the small sitting room, and as she watched him in Thomas's chair, had decided that the best place for the little portrait was at shoulder height to the right of the mantelpiece. Thomas merely had to raise his head to see it, and she, from her chair could see Thomas and the portrait with one glance.

Thomas's return was much delayed, and the waiting Charlotte became increasingly anxious about the recklessness of her action, and the length and depth of her deception. She wondered how many others knew of it and by what accident Mrs. Allen had let it be known. She tried to imagine his response if Thomas heard it from another source. Memory of the day revived her feelings of fear and uncertainty and the agonies she had concealed from him at the time. How could she explain all that? She could not broach the subject immediately on his return. He needed time to tell her anything he wanted to share about his meeting with the Dean, which may have been an important and serious event. His delay added to her anxiety. She simply wanted him to be at home, ignorant of the event so that she could confess, but did not know how she could bear to do it.

Ethel brought a lamp as the room darkened. Charlotte sat, tense and exhausted by misery, awaiting the sound of his horse. The effort to rise was almost beyond her and as she went slowly to greet him her eyes were fixed on his face but she could not read it. Was he chastened or exonerated, happy or unhappy? Her own face, however, was clearly as transparent as crystal. He put his great arm round her and led her into the little sitting room, closing the door behind them.

"What is it Charlotte? What has happened?" She told him, standing before him, eyes fixed straight ahead at the buttons on his chest. Told him what she had done and why she had done it, knowing that he could not approve, since it subverted the intentions of Lady Catherine. She had suffered for deceiving him but had not known how to undeceive him, until today when she had learned from her visitor that he might hear it from someone else. She was very sorry for her deception but he must understand that she could not be penitent for the action itself. She felt it no disloyalty to have preserved Mrs. Fountain and her child from a pauper dependency in the home of a callous and disregarding brother-in-law.

"Oh Thomas! I recognize and respect your devotion to Lady Catherine but please do not think less of me because I cannot share it." She could not raise her eyes to an unreadable face. He did not speak but stood very still, the buttons moved slightly away from her then back again, as she felt herself pressed firmly into his chest, the arms came round behind and his cheek rested on her head.

"Charlotte! I cannot bear that you should distress yourself on my account. Nothing could lessen my regard for you. You are everything to me."

The most beautiful sentences she had ever heard, echoed first in her head, then her heart and then suffused her completely. She thought, inexplicably, of the two sons of the ancient Greek priestess who, failing to find horses to do it, dragged their mother's chariot to the Shrine of the Goddess then expired on the spot, allowed to die in their moment of greatest happiness. How foolish! She then remembered with joy that the man whose arms now held her probably knew which goddess it was! Held in this wonderful extended embrace, she exonerated herself completely from any charge of having entrapped him. Her own love had come complete in a miraculous instant, Thomas's had grown towards it. Whose love was greater was irrelevant. They were right for each other.

CHAPTER

28

After the Service for Lord Grendon and the reception that followed it, Thomas and Charlotte came out of the great door at Rosings, descended the steps, and were walking away when she stopped suddenly and turned to look back at the entrance, the steps, the colonnaded portico, the doors. Thomas, curious, watched her.

"Even the largest doors are made to open Thomas, otherwise they would not be doors." She thought with affection of Mary Fountain and observed his expression; bemused with raised eyebrows.

"Thomas I'm too restless to go home, can we go for a walk?" His response was to veer to the left.

"Pleached Limes," he offered with a smile, nodding towards a receding line of trees that marked a broad walk. Thomas's relief that the Service was over was palpable; she shared it. She had so many impressions and memories that must be rendered into a coherent account for her mother. The service to satisfy a vainglorious Lady Catherine had given way to a modest farewell to a young life accidentally cut short. The Rosings chapel was plain white with graceful curves, outlined in pale wood, to a small dome. There were slender windows of stained glass, chiefly red and blue, but unreadable at a distance. Sir Lewis was tucked away in an apse at the East end. His image in a Roman toga, and longer she suspected than in life, lay on top of the tomb with room beside him for Lady Catherine.

The gathering afterwards had been in yet another huge room, new to Charlotte, with large carved sofas upholstered in blue brocade. A light repast, serviced by footmen satisfied the small gathering. The Dean had come to the service and brought the Archdeacon, and when Miss de Bourgh had thanked Thomas for a moving and comforting service, each of them had murmured their approval. Sir James Ayres greeted Charlotte and begged an introduction to her husband whose hand he shook heartily. Others present were those who had associated with the young man in the county or in London, for Miss de Bourgh had let it be known that all such would be welcome at the service. As they left the gathering Miss de Bourgh had enfolded both Thomas's hands into her own and thanked him again with a moving sincerity that touched Charlotte's heart.

Where the limes ceased, a choice of three paths tempted them.

"Retrace or continue?" He asked.

"Might you get lost?"

"Possibly."

"Retrace. I am ready now to continue my letter to Lucas Lodge. Are you content, Thomas, with the way the Service went?"

"Yes I am."

"It was just right. Miss de Bourgh was the good judge of that."

On the tray in the hall was a letter. She recognized the hand of Mary Fountain. She gave her outdoor clothes to Ethel and retired to the little sitting room, eager to read.

"Dear Mrs. Collins,

You have deserved a letter expressing my profound thanks much earlier than this. Please forgive me. I was so overflowing with the relief that your action had afforded me, that it delayed the shock that inevitably followed when I realized the harm that it might do to yourself and Mr. Collins. I do stress that I have never found Lady Catherine to be a vindictive woman but her anger towards me, inexplicable though I find it, was terrifying and intense. It is my worst nightmare now that she will turn it upon you. I have confided this fear to Lady Lucas (please forgive me for doing this) and she has agreed to collude with me in concealing the connection between my departure and yourself. She and I shall now be strangers unless our paths cross in the normal course of events. This, it pains me to write, must also be the situation if you and Mr. Collins visit. I have assured Lady Lucas that I had no contact with either your sister Maria or Miss Elizabeth Bennet during their stay at Rosings.

Your parents have provided us with a wonderful cottage, suitably modest and comfortably appointed. We have settled in most happily. My admiration for them is as boundless as is my gratitude.

You opened an escape route for me where none had existed and if Lady Catherine never learns of it, my fear will be groundless, but forgive me for feeling obliged to make it known. It also dictates that we must be strangers. I include no return address, forgive me, and know that my gratitude to you will be everlasting."

Charlotte read the letter a second time then laid it aside for Thomas to read. She would visit Mrs. Allen tomorrow, confident that Mrs. Fountain would not have severed that connection. She gave up all hope of continuing her letter home, picked up a shawl and made for the seat in the potting shed. He smiled at her but shook his head in disbelief that she should wish to be there. It was perfect. Thomas was content with his day and now totally absorbed transferring plants from small pots to larger pots. She watched him, swathed in sacking that was doing nothing to protect his clothing. She would provide herself with some unbleached linen and make him a sensible apron.

"She is not *your* patroness." Her mother's statement sprang into her mind, along with the enormity of the act that could wreak vengeance on Charlotte. Could Lady Catherine hate Mrs. Fountain so much that she would deprive Thomas of his benefice because Charlotte had helped her? Could she do that?

"Absolutely not!" The sensible part of her spoke firmly and aloud. Thomas raised his dead and she smiled at him, shaking her head. It disturbed her that her friend's opinion of Lady Catherine could have been brought so low as even to imagine her capable of such an act. Perhaps she was. She was grateful for her friend's forethought and decided not to show Thomas the letter.

29

As Charlotte prepared to leave for Mrs. Allen's house next morning Lady Catherine's coach went down the lane to Rosings. She sighed.

Mrs. Allen welcomed her warmly. She too, had heard from Mrs. Fountain and had considered herself a good channel for correspondence. She read aloud from Mrs. Fountain's own letter, her delight at the comfort and pleasantness of her new home and how, when she had commenced teaching letters to Lottie and Dorcas it had raised the interest of others and she was contemplating the possibility of a small school. Emotion overcame Mrs. Allen for she was missing Lottie, whom she had come to love. She had been reluctant to undertake the responsibility at her age but her nephew, himself a soldier, had persuaded her to meet mother and child and when Mrs. Fountain clearly and bravely explained her situation, she could not refuse. She had been aghast when Lady Catherine's action had instantly returned Mrs. Fountain to the situation she had worked so hard to avoid.

"And you Mrs. Collins! Mrs. Fountain wanted to tell you herself what had happened, which is why I sent Nell to fetch you back, but …. Forgive me, my Dear, I was at a loss when you intervened so surprisingly. I saw the cruel raising of hopes that could not be met. I was sure your husband could not allow it and felt obliged to share my fear with Mrs. Fountain. But, you see, I had forgot that he was that same kind man who had carried Lottie, asleep, miles on horseback to her mother the day of the great storm. But, my Dear, she was so still and quiet after you left us that day, that I was concerned for her. When she turned her face to me I could not read it. I can only describe it as a 'wondering' look, but she was comforted. She actually laughed.

"It is the answer," she said softly, "to a prayer I had not yet even formulated!" She smiled on Lottie who had looked up at her laugh. "Someone we love, who loves us has done it on our behalf Lottie, we must pray our thanks." Lottie smiled back and put her hands together as if it was a game.

I had to leave the room. She could only have meant her dead husband and since I had no real hope, I feared for her disappointment. When we came together again she said, "Mrs. Allen I have come to love you, and you have come to love Lottie, is it not good fortune that we are able to spend some little time together in your welcoming home? While we *are* together let us banish anxiety and practise affection."

It was a like a miracle when Lady Lucas's letter arrived. *Then* I could banish anxiety and practise affection. We fell on our knees in this room and thanked God. I confess I did the same again after I watched the coach drive off to Meryton."

The two ladies were so pleasant together that Charlotte accepted an invitation to the mid-day meal. She was very thoughtful when she left her friend, and did not remember the return of Lady Catherine until she reached the Parsonage in the afternoon.

"Ethel, I saw Lady Catherine arrive just before I left this morning."

"Not Lady Catherine ma'am. Her coach with Alice her maid and the groom. Stayed about three hours and left all packed up. Lady Catherine is going touring."

Charlotte had returned home for what had become an occasional special meeting at the kitchen table with Mrs. Wilby, the cook. The mutual embarrassment of their first encounter, had resolved into a mutual respect. The large shabby book that Charlotte took with her always received an affectionate pat from Mrs. Wilby, who brought to the table her own cornucopia of experience and ideas. Together they planned a meal for an exceptional occasion, as they had done for the first time while excluded from Rosings, and selected a dish for testing. Charlotte, seared by the embarrassing memory of Dorcas, was unwilling to ask the cook if she could read, and explained carefully everything that was written. Mrs.Wilby appeared to commit it to memory.

The dish chosen and discussion completed, Charlotte closed her book and rose from the table. She was very startled to hear Mrs.Wilby ask if she knew whether Mrs. Fountain was "all right."

"Mrs. Collins, we know she wouldn't go off like that without a word. We want her to know that, and how sorry we are, and to wish her well. Rumour is that you know where she's at, so they asked me to write to her and ask you if you would send it."

She produced the letter from her pocket and gave it to Charlotte. Mrs. Fountain's name, written in a fair hand, was the first line of an address. Charlotte looked at the letter, silenced momentarily by embarrassment.

"Yes. She will be pleased to have such a letter. I don't have her address, but I know someone who has."

"That would be Mrs. Allen, I suppose, who looked after the little girl."

Startled by this accurate assumption, Charlotte was half looking back when she collided in the hall with Mr. Darcy walking from the front door. She dropped her book. As it fell it hit the hat he held in his hand and both tumbled onto the floor at their feet.

"Mrs. Collins! I assure you it was not my intention to walk into your house and assault you with my hat. But you defended yourself, very ably, with a very large book."

Mr. Darcy was laughing without restraint. Charlotte had to laugh and Ethel was controlling her face with effort as she opened the door to the little sitting room. They had never heard Mr. Darcy laugh. Charlotte inquired after Colonel Fitzwilliam. They were joint travellers. On their way to London they had called at Rosings on a solicitous visit to their cousin Anne, who had been unable to attend the funeral. The Colonel was taking the opportunity to visit a friend in the neighbourhood. Mrs. Collins could expect him shortly.

Charlotte indicated a seat and Mr. Darcy sat, then catching sight of the little portrait facing him rose to stand before it.

"Is she not lovely? It is Mr. Collins' mother."

Mr. Darcy's sympathetic face as he looked back at her, led her to confide.

"I have just persuaded him to allow me to hang it. He has kept it in a box since he was a child."

"Yes. She is very lovely."

He resumed his seat and told her that his cousin had spoken very warmly of Mr. Collins' service in the Rosings Chapel. She had been very grateful that he not only conducted the service, but had been the one to suggest it in the first place. Charlotte was considering that statement, when a commotion in the hall announced the arrival of Colonel Fitzwilliam. She saw her own expression of surprise reflected in the face of Mr. Darcy, and they both rose as the door opened to admit him. The Colonel's face and demeanour spoke determination.

CHAPTER

30

Within minutes of the Colonel's entry, courtesies had been exchanged, Mr. Darcy had set off for Rosings and Charlotte and the Colonel were seated facing each other over the small table. The embarrassment Charlotte had anticipated of not knowing by what name to address him, had evaporated before a more important discomforting sense that the control of her home had passed away from herself to someone else, and that 'someone else' was not her husband. This could not be right. She stood. Surprised, he too rose. They faced each other.

"Colonel Fitzwilliam, am I your prisoner?" His astonished burst of laughter was very loud. He suppressed it. He assured her that she was not. A right balance restored she sat, invited him to do the same and asked the purpose of his visit, for clearly he had one and her unexpected question had not deflected him.

"I have come directly to you from Mrs. Allen of Hutton. It seems that you alone can tell me what I require to know, the whereabouts of Mary Fountain. I tell you, in confidence, why I require to know. A communication was sent to her recently. It was of such great importance to her that it had been my intention to deliver it in person, but my brother's death dictated otherwise. The communication demands her personal response, but she has not responded. It indicated a source of substantial funds. She has made no move to access them. Lady Catherine says she is with her sister. I know that she is not. All this gives me cause for alarm. Charles Fountain was my friend. I must know that his wife and his child are safe. I will be convinced that they are safe only when I can see them, to do that I must find them." She stared into his determined face, then looked away quickly before he might read her perception that behind his anxiety there lay a very deep personal attachment.

"She cannot have received it."

She told him of the day she had visited Mrs. Allen and found Mrs. Fountain there, and heard the shocking news of her dismissal. He listened, silent and grim faced. His look changed to one of incredulity as she told him what had followed. She took Mary Fountain's letter from her writing desk and handed it to him. He read it quickly and then a second time, intently.

"You observe she withheld her address but you can go to Meryton, a town in Hertfordshire known to Mr. Darcy and find my mother, Lady Lucas. If you ask her to take you to the cottage, you will find Mrs. Fountain and Lottie."

He settled back into his seat, looking fixedly at her. Tenseness and anxiety dissolved from him, but relief did not make him happy. It made him thoughtful, pinch-faced.

"Your letter sets my mind at ease about their safety and well-being. It worries me that you think she has not received the communication. I see no reason to bother her now but may have good reason to do so when I inquire further into the matter."

He stood, then walked about the small room like a man requiring a larger space.

"Please forgive me if I was overbearing, it was unintentional. Circumstances have had me by the ears since the death of my brother. I presume that you and Mrs. Fountain will communicate through Mrs. Allen? Do tell her of our conversation, though it is partly good news and partly bad. We must hope that she will excuse me for discussing her private affairs, I saw no alternative."

He stood before her smiling, and she rose.

"You are quite small Mrs. Collins, but I do not think I would attempt to take you prisoner unless I had reinforcements." They laughed together. She extended her hand, which he shook, then departed, still smiling.

She was by the drawing room window next morning, opening her little writing desk, when the Colonel and Mr. Darcy passed on horseback bound for London. She knew they could not see her but they seemed to salute the Parsonage as they went by.

These two young men had much to bind them in loyalty and affection. Their mothers had found a mutual accord on meeting as sisters-in-law, and it had deepened into the firmest of friendships. The early death of one of them had generated in the other a transfer of love to the bereft child, and with the co-operation of his father, she had ensured frequent and often lengthy contacts between the boys.

Differences of temperament, character and prospects had made each interesting to the other. Darcy, an only son, serious, reflective and conserving, had grown and matured into the beneficial management of his inherited estates in Derbyshire. Fitzwilliam, active and unruly second son of a profligate Earl, whose only advice to his sons was to marry a fortune, had accepted a Commission purchased by his mother and made for himself an interesting life in the army. Personal misfortunes had given each a further understanding of the other. Darcy, after a previous stay at Rosings, had unburdened himself about a proposal of marriage he had made to Miss Elizabeth Bennet that should have been most gratefully accepted, but had been rejected with a humiliating and angry response.

Fitzwilliam had confessed to a similar proposal, made by himself, that had not only been rejected by the lady, but she had reprimanded him for making it at all! Each of them had been scorched and singed, but neither had been cured; the rejection had tempered and refined the emotion. More recently Darcy, having embarked on a knightly quest to free his unresponsive lady from the family disgrace of a scandalous elopement, had sought aid from his cousin to identify and purchase, for the delinquent absconders, a military commission sufficiently remote from the family to ensure the rarest of visits.

They were now bound for the London mansion of Fitzwilliam's mother, the Countess of Raimond, always a welcoming home to both of them. Much of Society spoke of the Earl of Raimond with disparagement and disapproval of his rakish lifestyle. The Countess of Raimond was not one of them. His generosity at the time of the birth of their second son, in returning to her one quarter of her dowry, had won him a lifetime's regard. They had not been frequently in each other's company for some years but, when they were, politeness and affection ruled. The sudden death of their child had added a further quality, as the deep raging anger of the father had given way before the profound quiet grief of the mother. She was to remain a further two days at Gavelston.

Charlotte, aware that they could not see her, still raised an arm to acknowledge their salute, then bent to her task; to tell Mary Fountain of her change of fortune and of the Colonel's concern at what he thought was her disappearance. She hesitated. Her own recent perception that personal feelings had dictated his action, must be concealed. She wrote of all that he had disclosed to her, and the depth of his anxiety, and all that she had disclosed to him. She felt it no exaggeration to describe the relief she had witnessed, but refrained from mentioning her own sense of his personal disappointment at not finding the one he sought.

"He said it was not necessary to 'bother' you with a personal visit though I would have given him your address if I had had it. He will only 'bother' you when he discovers something further."

Having signed the letter she read it through carefully. It seemed very stiff. She heard herself heave a deep sigh and laughed at the sound. She knew what she knew. The pain of Cupid's dart was deep. She pitied the Colonel. She had both relieved and frustrated him. His search had led him not to Mary Fountain, but to Charlotte Collins, and she could do nothing to relieve a disappointment tinged with that dreadful malady, Lovesickness. She picked up her pen and wrote carefully.

"We both know that had he given you the news himself, he would have witnessed your relief and joy, and been rewarded with your thanks. Imparting it through me deprives him of that pleasure. What a pity!" She folded and sealed the letter and returned it to her box.

32

"Imparting it through me deprives him of that pleasure. What a pity!" The two-weeks-old letter lay on Mary Fountain's lap. She had it by heart. That she was a moderately independent woman again flooded her with relief. That he saw no reason to 'bother' her made her sad.

She recalled the mistrust she had felt towards him before they met, when newly married to Major Charles Fountain she had moved into the world of his friends and learned of the 'joke' that if you knew an heiress you must introduce her to Colonel Fitzwilliam, as his father had instructed him to marry one. She had disapproved of such frivolity. FitzWilliam seemed to have sensed some antipathy at their first meeting, for he appeared to elude subsequent opportunities to be in her presence, and when that was unavoidable their conversations were polite and brief. Sensible Charles had shaken his head at her prejudice and given the colonel his total trust and friendship, a most unlikely friendship, between infantryman and cavalryman, that had arisen from a mutual interest in the Rifle Brigade with its superior weapon and tactics. Charles had followed his interest to the logical conclusion. Fitzwilliam, having wavered, could not bear to part from his horse.

The Colonel had investigated the circumstances of her husband's death. When he sought her out, after some months to disclose them, he had been visibly shocked to find her in drastically reduced circumstances and totally speechless at the existence of Lottie. He had offered marriage and been refused with an anger and stiffness that shocked him. She grew warm at the memory of that occasion. She had been surprised at the heat of her own anger, wracked by the degrading conviction that he had proposed out of pity, and found relief in her refusal. That eruption between them had not diminished his continuing active concern for the welfare of mother and child. It persisted even when her embarrassment at their near poverty made her wish that he would desist. He was always impersonal and detached, but his questioning was direct and pertinent. In time, she appreciated this, responded in kind, and discovered Charles's friend.

Charles had told him, he reported, that her sister was the wife of a substantial landowner in Berkshire, and she could make her home with them in the event of his death. Why had she not done so?

She had a dislike of the man and would go there only as a last resort. She had never made this known to Charles.

She understood, she had told him, that her husband's original commission, a captaincy in the Foot Guards, would be sold to reimburse her, and there would be, also, a pension for the widow of a major. When would this happen?

He had shaken his head. He was powerless to intervene in any financial matters but he suspected their resolution was slow. What other resources did she have?

Hardly any, as he could see from their situation. She must exploit her education. A governess seemed the only option.

"A governess!"

His formality and detachment had disappeared in an explosive cry of horrified disbelief that startled her. It had made her smile and he had responded, but warily.

Yes. But she would not take Lottie into such a situation. The little girl, with a nursemaid, must be independently and satisfactorily housed nearby. Her resources were sufficient to meet that cost.

It was from this moment that Mary Fountain acknowledged to herself a deep tenderness for Colonel Fitzwilliam. His re-action had been extra-ordinary but she did not doubt that it was genuine. His eyes remained on her face as he rubbed his chin slowly backwards and forwards with his thumb. His gaze moved to the corner of the ceiling as his right hand took hold of his left lapel then his head came slowly down to allow his thumb to move slowly backwards and forwards over his lips. It was a physical demonstration of a man deep in thought; thought concentrated on her; glancing at her, but not seeing her. She hoped, with all her heart, that he would not say anything to embarrass either of them.

"What about a Housekeeper?"

She had laughed aloud in a surprise that infected him, and they laughed together without quite knowing why. Then, when the laughter subsided but good nature remained, he told her about a house called Rosings in Kent. He thought the housekeeper was looking to retire when she had trained a successor. It was a substantial household and a serious commitment. It would be demanding but secure and would carry far more respect than would a governess.

He could not approve her doing it. She would be a servant, abandoning all claim to status in her present lifetime relationships. Did she realize that? He himself was an occasional visitor to Rosings, and from childhood had formed a friendship with the present housekeeper. A similar friendship with herself would be impossible, and though he would always be a friend to Lottie and herself there could, during his visits, be no friendliness between them. Would that offend her?

What would her sister think of such an act? Would her only relation tolerate it? What about her sister's husband? Might they perhaps cut her off? Would it not be better to accept life in the home of an unpopular, avoidable brother-in-law and hope for an improvement in life's prospects, than to suffer such a drastic fall in status for herself and the risk that it posed for Lottie?

Not when that brother-in-law had been a suitor whose offer of marriage she had refused and who had taken offence at her refusal. He looked at her very hard.

"You must be quite sure that this is what you want?"

"I am quite sure." She was smiling with relief. "And very grateful."

She stroked the letter and opened her eyes. The image of Dorcas hung before her, and beyond Dorcas, was the face of Colonel Fitzwilliam.

"We heard the bell in the garden Ma'am, was you asleep?"

"Clearly not asleep, day-dreaming perhaps." Said the colonel.

She stood joyfully and held out both her hands to welcome him. He took them but released them immediately.

He had no good news for her. They stood in silence at the window of the little room. Their eyes followed Dorcas and Lottie as they moved in play at the farthest end of the garden but their minds were elsewhere, their faces grave. The Colonel had related how a Lieutenant of the 95th, had presented himself at Rosings on his behalf, to deliver a dispatch to Mrs. Fountain. He had been taken, not to Mrs. Fountain, but to Lady Catherine who had received him graciously. When he repeated the purpose of his visit, she became very chill. She had said that Mrs. Fountain was not available to see him but that he may leave the package and indicated a table. She then dismissed him. He had repossessed the dispatch, telling her that if he could not give it to Mrs. Fountain he could only exchange it for the seal, or signature, of a responsible person. Lady Catherine had been very displeased but he had not moved. Ink and pen were brought, Lady Catherine had signed, indicated the table again and he had placed the dispatch upon it and left with the signed receipt. The horse had been extended every courtesy, the rider none.

Lady Catherine, challenged by Colonel Fitzwilliam, had denied all knowledge of the incident. The dispatch was missing.

Mary Fountain recalled the brief and shocking interview with Lady Catherine; a reason at last, that was some relief. She pushed it from her mind. What action could she take to retrieve the situation? This was the question she intended to ask as she turned to face him.

"Colonel Fitzwilliam …" She hesitated. "Is that still your name? How do you wish me to address you?"

"As Husband." His private thought spoke itself. Still turning, she stopped in surprise. He took a step backwards.

"Forgive me. You have given me an answer and I respect it. I remain Colonel Fitzwilliam Ma'am."

He stood before her, out of uniform, erect like a soldier, his face solemn and pink with embarrassment. She felt a sudden bursting of relief and heat within herself, took his hand to her own burning cheek and then rested her other palm against his, feeling his warmth.

"We are like children." she said. "Oh, my good friend! How I have come to love you!"

He took her hands towards his chest and held them. He was speechless and when he was able to speak it was as though forcing the words out of himself.

"Did you think I led Charles into extravagance? I did not know …."

She pressed her fingers over his lips.

"Charles Fountain was not a man to be led where he did not wish to go." She smiled. "I could not know what *was* extravagance. What I also could not know was how short his life would be. I cherish everything in it that made him happy. Your friendship came high in that regard and I begrudged nothing, not then and not now."

He looked on her face, remembering the first time he saw her, a supremely happy bride on the arm of his friend. He had broken the commandment and coveted his friend's wife. He held her close, speaking softly over her head.

"I never sought a fortune but fate has given me something priceless."

CHAPTER

33

Colonel Fitzwilliam was stony faced. He stood behind and to the left of his father, who sat on a gilded chair on a dais, in state, in the grand salon at Gavelston.

He had asked the Earl's permission to marry Mrs. Fountain and it had been refused. He had told him of his intention to marry her and been dismissed. He had been obliged to meet Ramsden, the Earl's Agent. He, a man of business, had taken from a leather case three sheets of closely written paper and introduced him to three heiresses one of whom Grendon was to have chosen for his wife. He explained, simply but earnestly, that revenue from Raimond estates and investments was insufficient to sustain a lifestyle suitable to an Earl. It was the duty of each heir to marry an heiress. The heiress was to be the only child, carefully nurtured and reared for High Society, of a commoner rich and ambitious enough to purchase a noble title for his grandson.

Replacing the sheets in the case he had put it into the hand of the Colonel who had left it on the table and gone to seek a meeting with his father. He told the Earl of his intention to marry Mary Fountain.

The death of his older son had ravaged the Earl of Raimond and he had not concealed the depth of his grief and anger. The anger was directed equally at his own leniency and at his adored son's evasive reluctance to tie himself into matrimony. The grief was overwhelming. The shocking spectacle of the lofty demanding Egoist collapsing into help-less dependency had terrified his household. A plea to the Countess had brought her to Gavelston and he had emerged from her care physically weaker, less angry but still consumed by grief. FitzWilliam, who had not witnessed the collapse, had marked the physical change but recog-nized at once the unchanged implacable will. Affection was immaterial, respect was ingrained, obedience also. The Earl had agreed to receive the woman, but only in the ludicrously formal, full dress, circumstances. There would be no festivity, no relaxation of mourning.

The journey north to Gavelston was two days by coach. FitzWilliam's first rebellious decision was to marry and present his father with a fait accompli. His mother counselled against it and her argument was per-suasive. The blow to his father would be like a second death. She doubted his mind could withstand it and it would set them asunder. She had no wish to be forced into a choice between husband and son. He must accept his father's decision, making the journey as comfortable as possible. She could not put her own coach to his use, since it would be recognized, but she was sure she could borrow one equivalent to it and allow him four men she would use herself for such a journey. She assumed he would accompany it on horseback. She understood his determination to marry but was against the fait accompli. If he married without his father's con-sent he must still tell him face to face where the ceremony was to be held and invite him to attend. He had left her house persuaded and set himself to arranging the journey.

The Countess had taken a moment to remember her own Presentation, when she and her parents had left their own comfort-able home to endure, for three days, the draughty inconveniences of Gavelston; the culmination of a plan of her father, a cynical sardonic man, but curiously loveable. Disappointed in his expectation of a son to inherit his vast and increasing fortune and found a dynasty, he had looked speculatively at that inferior investment, his daughter. He saw a bright, handsome child with curiosity and determination and decided to continue an existing dynasty by purchasing a grandson who would inherit nobility. His wife, an educated woman with remote aristocratic connections, thought a family seeking such a connection required a higher polish than their own, and canvassed the Grand Tour as a beginning to the polishing process. Surprised by her acuity he had left the polishing in her hands and been impressed by her ability to detect and deflect the poseur and the parasite. Over the years there had been, periodically, tutor/guests who had lived and dined with the family, polishing demeanour and manners; expanding an understanding of European painting, sculpture and architecture and the history of their own country. In the course of three Grand Tours they had sat patiently and quietly through operas and chamber concerts in a variety of European cities while others had been less polite. The child had taken to the life, absorbing its benefits. She had noticed that whereas her mother seemed unchanged, her father had altered beyond recognition into a polite and considerate husband and father.

Presented on the first evening, in a gown exquisite but not flamboyant, she had dipped a courtesy to the seated Earl and received a smiling response and warm welcome. The heir, Lord Grendon, had stood behind and to the left of the Earl, who introduced them quite casually with a gesture over his shoulder. The young man's face, surprisingly handsome, was like a stone. Aware that she had looked at him with smiling admiration she deliberately closed her face down to a look of equal coldness and barely returned the nod he had given her before rejoining her parents. Her shrewd father had observed the young man. "We're inspecting the Merchandise." He whispered covertly. "We don't like it we don't buy it. We do not truckle,"

The visit had been festive, sociable and luxuriously clad. She had ignored the young man and no-one had obliged them to converse but she was aware that he hovered close. Tutored to recognize sophistication, she had not found it common in the company. She was pleased at the opportunity to demonstrate her fluency in Italian as she discussed the mosaics in the tomb of Galla Placidia with a guest who was a native of

Ravenna, keeping her voice always low and modest. Eventually she had found the young man standing before her with his beautiful solemn face.

"I hope to God my sisters like you!" He had spoken with marked expressiveness and real anxiety. She had not heard of any sisters. She had paused for thought and told him that was not necessary. It was just necessary that they each liked the other. He laughed aloud.

"Well of course we do. We are to be married." He was like an oversized child, and not quite clean. There had been no more talk of Merchandise. Her mother had called it a dynastic marriage, and of course she understood.

After the marriage she had dipped and floated for a year in the bear-garden that was Gavelston, and in or around the London residence, finding friendship with Anne, uneasy exchanges with Catherine and intrigued but never moved by the beautiful inexpressive over grown child husband. Then there had come the miraculous transformation that children brought, when her huge love had embraced the whole world cocooning even the husband on the edge with tenderness. She had felt empowered, identified her own small household at Gavelston and uplifted it, minus the cocoon, for visits of up to a month at a time in her much more civilized and comfortable home where her mother had raised an eyebrow while her father purred over his young lions.

Mary Fountain, having entered the Earl's home to a reception of meticulous courtesy but no trace of welcome, had met the clear but unexpressed view that her child was an unexpected, unwelcome superfluity that must be disposed of before the Presentation could proceed.

She had already fought and won two skirmishes. The first, quite brief, was for an appropriate and private place where she could make sure that Lottie was comfortable. The second, rather longer, was in her resistance to all persuasion to separate mother and child, and leave the child with a stranger, while the mother was presented to the Earl. The latter engagement had been so protracted, that she had instructed the leading tormentor to go instantly to Lord Grendon, inform him that she was about to leave the premises and required his immediate attendance. Her will had prevailed but she no illusions that anything better was to follow.

A footman led them down a wide corridor with huge windows on the left and a series of open rooms on the right towards closed double doors at the end. The footman, informed that the Earl was waiting, had set off at some speed. Mrs. Fountain refusing to rush Lottie, watched the doors open and heard herself announced while several yards from the threshold. This confirmed her opinion that footmen, though generally handsome, were not to be relied upon for good sense. A further surprise awaited her upon the threshold, the room was a larger version of the Great Salon at Rosings. Lady Catherine had reproduced it in detail. Concealing heightened sensibilities with an assumed calm she paused, gave Lottie's hand a reassuring squeeze and pointed out to her the presence of Colonel FitzWilliam. She walked at the child's pace towards an enthroned black clad figure, noticing with her Housekeeper's eye, a slovenly slipped swag on one of the great window curtains. She stopped and looked up into the face of the seated man who had mercilessly scarified his indiscreet sister and was now poised to administer a *coup de grace* to an unacceptable daughter in law. She recognized a familial resemblance to Lady Catherine, refined into an overall symmetry; it was the ravaged face of what had been a very beautiful man. Distracted by his attire of knee breeches, diamond buttons and a good deal of fine black lace, she was glad to raise her eyes and rest them on the face of a man, in magnificent dress uniform with a touch of mourning, who seemed not to resemble his father in any respect.

The Earl was astonished to see her enter the room holding a child by the hand. He watched her approach, affronted that she had brought a child, affronted that she was unaccompanied by a serving woman and affronted that her attire was inadequate to the occasion. He had never demeaned himself to interview a governess. Her dark eyes looked straight at him as she stopped moving then left his face and moved to meet those of the son behind him. Face and eyes softened as she greeted him in silence. No-on looked at him like that. Had anyone ever? Not the son he had adored; his re-incarnated self, willful, daring, reckless and dead.

"Sir, may I present Mrs. Fountain, widow of my friend Charles Fountain."

He nodded, unsmiling.

"Mrs. Fountain."

She nodded in return, formal, unsmiling.

"Sir."

He sensed non-compliance. She was as reluctant for this meeting as he was himself and did not conceal it. He grew impatient with the charade, felt an intense surge of anger against the defiant son who had forced this upon him, who had survived his quicksilver brother and now brought this unsympathetic creature to affront his dignity. He made no attempt to restrain it.

"My son tells me you are so desirous of being a Countess that you would condemn him to a life of penury."

He ignored his son's gasp of protest. Watched her eyes widen and mouth open at the shocking discourtesy.

Mary Fountain felt distinctly light headed. Wearing the most expensive dress she had owned during the period of her mourning, she realized that she had never in her life owned a gown in any cloth or colour that would have been adequate to this occasion, in this room. She had come dressed for, and expecting, a beheading, but the dreaded coup-de-grace had been an angry bleat about penury from a man seated in a gilded chair and dressed in lace and diamonds. She shifted her gaze to a son deeply offended by his father and spoke to him, softly, and almost smiling in amusement.

"If you think he told you that Sir, you have misled yourself."

FitzWilliam's eyebrows rose higher as his face resolved from shocked indignation to disbelief.

The silent Earl thought fleetingly and surprisingly of his own Countess, a woman of considerable wit and self-possession. His anger slid away. He had intended to meet the woman, instruct his son to take her for his mistress and marry the fortune. That horse would not run. They would marry anyway, he had no power to prevent it, why weary himself with attempts to thwart it. She already had a child, an heir was more important than a fortune and this son took no risk other than a refusal to resign his commission. Perhaps a soldier's widow could be more persuasive than a father. He broke the silence.

"Of course he said no such thing." He rose and walked towards her calling to his son as he did so. "Major Fountain? A hussar?"

"No Sir. A Major of the 95th Rifles."

"Ah! A marksman!" His interest was engaged. The child was staring up at him. He extended a lace cuffed hand to touch her head but she would not permit it and folded backwards round her mother.

"Mrs. Fountain." He took her free hand and leading her to a gilded sofa, invited her to sit and sat also. "You lost your husband in the Peninsular? Were you able to discover the circumstances of his death?"

"I think so, with the help of Colonel FitzWilliam."

"Can you bear to speak of it?"

"I am glad to. Brave men deserve that we speak of them at every opportunity. He was badly wounded early in the retreat. He was carried on a hurdle as they retreated throughout the night and during the night he died. The terrain they passed through was impossible for a quick burial and they were hard pressed. Later in the morning they came upon a softer landscape and two burial parties fell out to inter, as quickly as possible my husband and another soldier. Where he is buried I do not know and suspect it would be impossible to discover. My consolation is the knowledge that he *was* buried; deep enough, with some dignity and appropriate rites."

A soldier's widow with a calm account of what she hoped had happened. His son had moved alongside her, the child's hand transferred to his. They were already a family. If he would not resign his commission the sooner they married the better. He spoke to both of them.

"You cannot marry in the Chapel. Gavelston is in mourning for year. Arrange something quiet in London. Consult the Countess. Let me know." He rose. "Mrs. Fountain." He gave her a slight bow nodded to his son and, turning away, walked his diamond buckled shoes to a second pair of great double doors that were opened by a pair of footmen who closed them silently behind him.

They looked at each other. He was still half disbelieving, half laughing.

"Well done!" He said. "Well done!"

He picked up Lottie and they left the house of mourning, pausing only to adjust the offending swag on a window curtain.

CHAPTER

35

Charlotte walked from the Parsonage door along the lane to the wooden bench and sat. A tiny niggling anxiety regarding the soul of Mary Fountain's husband had grown to possess so great a part of her mind that she could no longer disregard it. She had almost told it to Thomas but decided it might be worth a few minutes on the Thinking Bench. There were three events she should consider, in reverse order of occurrence, for the most recent was the one that had raised the alarm.

Mrs. Allen had implied that Mrs. Fountain, when Charlotte mentioned her house in Meryton, had assumed some spiritual intervention from her late husband.

She, herself, on the day of the incident had had a flashing thought of the powerless dead father.

Thomas had, on that famous occasion weeks ago, confronted Lady Catherine on behalf of a soul 'in peril'.

Charlotte wished she knew more about souls. That of young Lord Grendon had caused Thomas serious anxiety. She had witnessed it and could not doubt its importance. A soul was vulnerable between leaving the body and arriving in Heaven. 'Paradiso'. Her mind had revived an old memory. Senor Goldoni (Hams, Olive Oils and Cheese) on a visit to her father, in the old house in Meryton had found her with her head in a book and inquired what she read. It was stories of the Court of King

Arthur. He was a humorous gentleman, he had laughed and shaken a cautioning finger and asked if she knew the story of Francesca da Rimini. Of course she did not and was avid to know it. He had told her of the beautiful young Francesca, and Paolo, a handsome younger brother of her husband, who, reading those stories of Guinevere and Lancelot, fell so tragically in love that they had betrayed her husband and had been killed by him. The famous Dante Alhigieri had seen their souls in a vision, being flung constantly hither and thither by violent winds in Inferno, which is what he called Hell. She had never thought to ask if the famous Dante Alhigieri had seen Francesca's husband because he certainly should have been there also. The only other tormented soul she had heard of was Judas Iscariot, allowed one day of mercy in the year to cool himself on an ice floe.

She frowned and drew her mind firmly back. A soul in Hell could not escape. Could a soul in Heaven take leave of absence to interfere on behalf of the living? Quite bewildered she crystalised the real question that troubled her and asked it aloud.

"Do I believe that the soul of Major Fountain possessed me for a second when I offered my house?" Presented like that, the whole thing sounded so silly, the response was immediate.

"Absolutely not." She sighed with relief. She was glad that Mrs. Fountain, for whatever reason, had found immediate ease from the burden of her anxieties. She was also glad she had not mentioned anything of this to Thomas.

A tuft of grass moved almost imperceptibly nearby but she could not see the small mammal that caused it. There often seemed to be a lot going on around her, and in the hedge behind her. She had, on one occasion, seen a disappearing tail as she sat still and quiet. As for the Major, the powerless husband and father, she had certainly thought of him and felt for him. He had touched her heart, and she was glad.

As she walked more slowly home to the Parsonage her mind turned to Anne de Bourgh about whose secret depths she had long speculated. She sensed, with sympathy, that those depths had been carelessly and cruelly ploughed. Lady Catherine seemed not to have entertained a thought that Anne had both the right and the obligation to attend the funeral of her old playmate and much loved cousin Lord Grendon. Mr. Darcy, the Colonel and Sir James, all no doubt remembering her past illness, had supposed her indisposed and unable to travel to Gavelston. Miss de Bourgh had not disabused them. Charlotte, however, thought that Lady Catherine, eaten up by chagrin at the Earl's reprimand and threat, had simply overlooked her daughter's existence. Had it not been for Lady Catherine's earlier angry outburst, and Thomas's intervention, there would not have been a service for Anne to attend at all. She suspected that this neglect of a daughter's feelings might not be new. This time, however, there had been consequences.

Anne de Bourgh had presided over the reception following the service in Rosings Chapel, and done it with a sober unselfconscious dignity that had obliged her to raise her normally submissive head. The raised eyes had observed a minor incident between two footmen and she had sent a letter to the Rosings Steward mentioning this and requiring information of a new Housekeeper. He had replied, addressing her as 'Dear Miss Anne' and informed her that as Lady Catherine had not made him aware of any reason for Mrs. Fountain's absence, nor instructed him to replace her, perhaps her return was expected. He would await Lady Catherine's instruction. In frustration she had sent an appeal for advice to the previous Housekeeper, Mrs. White, and that old lady had responded in person bringing with her a widowed niece as an aid. These two women together were now, answerable to Miss de Bourgh, effectively restoring threads that had loosened and ravelled during the interregnum. The tacit approval of the household for an intervention that had put an end to general unease, uncertainty and some acrimonious squabbling, showed itself in a manifest new deference and respect, to which she had responded with enhanced confidence.

She continued the practice of entertaining the Parson and his wife to dinner. The deep pleasures of well informed and frequently amusing conversation, nourished Charlotte and she participated, not hesitating to ask questions which Thomas or Mrs. Jenkinson were happy to answer. Miss de Bourgh increasingly, did the same. She showed a real curiosity about Lucas Lodge and Charlotte's family. Since this was the easiest topic in the world about which to converse Charlotte indulged it. At dinner on one occasion, while referring to an aspect of their own dining room at the Parsonage, it had seemed the most natural thing in the world to suggest that the two ladies should see it for themselves. Why, she wondered, should they not dine there? As she hesitated she met a stare from Mrs. Jenkinson who appeared to will her to do it. Including Thomas with a gesture, she made that suggestion on their behalf and awaited the onslaught of the black cat but found instead a delighted acceptance. With that direct glance it seemed to Charlotte that she and Mrs. Jenkinson had formed a fanciful alliance to nourish Miss de Bourgh's bourgeoning confidence into a sturdy independence.

The success of the dinner party at the Parsonage was complete. Miss de Bourgh had arrived in a state of suppressed excitement, eyes shining and lips smiling, and Charlotte realized what a handsome young woman she was when happy. Dinner, (Mrs. Wilby interpreting Lady Lucas's recipes through the lens of her own experience) was superb. Time passed in the friendliest good humour and Charlotte was gratified that her guests had dressed to Rosings standard to honour the Parsonage dining room.

She had breathed a contented sigh as the door closed behind them and turned to find Thomas smiling behind her. He opened his arms and she walked her cheek to the buttons on his chest, and his arms came round behind. He spoke over her head.

"When you were a child did you never see a doll's house and wish you could get into it?"

The increasing speed of change in Miss de Bourgh seemed to bundle Charlotte along within it. In a period of only one month she had accompanied Charlotte on two Parish visits where, as Thomas had implied, she had been half expected and therefore added an extra relish to the occasion. Also, in the same time, the usual little dining party, with the addition of Sir James Ayers, had dined at Rosings, at the Parsonage, and finally at the home of Sir James himself. This latest dinner, had been particularly enjoyable as Miss de Bourgh and Sir James recalled family visits to the premises, involving not only themselves but also Grendon, Darcy and Fitzwilliam. They laughed without restraint at an episode that had involved Sir Lewis, when a mail gauntlet from the suit of armour in the hall, detached by the boys in accidental mischief and concealed under a carpet by Anne, had landed him in Lady Catherine's lap. It seemed that she, youngest smallest and slowest, was always running behind trying to put things right to protect them from the beatings that followed their mis-demeanours. They seemed, sadly, to agree that generally it had been Grendon who had the whippings.

Charlotte recalled their first meeting when Sir James had seemed to regret the severance of the family connection. She concluded his regret had been genuine, she smiled to herself, perhaps even heartfelt.

36

During her absence Lady Catherine's coach and servants had twice returned to Rosings to deposit and collect her effects. This morning the horn sounded in the lane. Lady Catherine was aboard.

Charlotte was engrossed in a letter from Lady Lucas, which included news of the Bennet family. The scandalous Lydia, who had become the honest Mrs. Wickham, was already the toast of the unsophisticated Northern garrison and was begging the family to visit her and witness her triumph. The horn sounded again. She laid her letter aside for a moment, remembering that Lizzie herself had been infatuated with Wickham the night of the Netherfield ball. The night she, herself, fell lovesick.

Lady Lucas mentioned that Mr. Bingley had returned to Netherfield. One of his guests had been Colonel Fitzwilliam whose name Maria remembered from her visit to Charlotte. His stay had been very brief. Was it possible that he, his circumstances having changed, and having met Elizabeth at the time of their visit, could have discovered her home and come to Netherfield with her in mind? Mrs. Bennet had grasped at this straw. Maria seemed to think this *might* be so and Lady Lucas had warned her daughter against stoking the fires of Mrs. Bennet's imagination. Charlotte wondered how she could save Lizzie from embarrassment by letting her know that the colonel's affections were engaged elsewhere, but concluded that she could not. It was a matter of regret to Charlotte that she and Lizzie did not correspond, but she knew that circumstances had made it impossible and resigned herself. She felt, however, she could now be sure that the colonel and Mary Fountain had met, and she must patiently wait to learn the outcome.

When Ethel brought her mid-day meal she was brimming with news or, Charlotte stifled the uneasy thought, gossip. Yesterday a soldier had presented himself at the London house to inquire for Lady Catherine. Told she was not at home he said he would return next morning. On being told of this Lady Catherine had, at the earliest opportunity, quit the house and returned to Rosings. (Ethel had this from the groom who had overseen the officer's mount.) On arrival at Rosings she had stumbled as she left the coach and been aided to her apartments and she had not left them.

Thomas returning home via Rosings reported that Lady Catherine, feeling unwell in London, had decided to recover at home. He had this from Mrs. Jenkinson who had urged him back to the Parsonage.

Three days later Lady Catherine was still confined to her apartments, visited only by Mrs. Jenkinson and Mrs. White. Ethel, bringing Charlotte her mid-day meal, told her that Edgar the groom had seen a mounted officer ride down to Rosings early in the morning and no one had seen him return. Charlotte reminded Ethel that many people passed both ways in the lane without being noticed.

Thomas, returning via Rosings in the late afternoon, reported that Mrs. White was at a loss as to what would be suitable accommodation for a military dispatch rider who had called to see her Ladyship. When told that she was too unwell to be disturbed, he had announced that it was not actually necessary to see her, but duty obliged him to remain until he could retrieve the dispatch that he had left in her possession. He said that failure to do so might result in a court-martial for mislaying a dispatch in time of war. This startling turn of events had put the Housekeeper, and therefore the house, into the grip of a mild panic. Charlotte, recalling the purpose of Colonel Fitzwilliam's earlier visit to her, related it to her husband. Their conclusion that this could be the same package was interesting but not useful. Charlotte smiled to herself. She knew she could rely upon Thomas to be alert in the matter.

CHAPTER

37

Lady Catherine was exhausted. The mention of a court martial had rallied the remnants of her energy only to dissipate them in hopelessness. Moist eyed and supported by cushions on a chaise longue by the great window of her apartments she gazed down over the garden and languidly visited the trail of her misfortunes. The death of her nephew had put her at odds with everything that made her life agreeable. Her curiosity to discover the circumstances of his death, had brought from her brother a swift and brutal reprimand that had licked and scorched friends of a lifetime, perhaps permanently estranging them. She had assumed that his change of mind about her attendance at the funeral had been an act of reconciliation. She was wrong. He had neither met her eye, nor addressed a single word to her during her stay and she had left immediately afterwards without a farewell. She mourned now for the dead nephew, but mourned even more the lost affection of the younger brother to whom she had turned for solace when upbraided by their older sister. That bond, sealed in childhood, had seemed impregnable but was now broken and she had already begun to wonder whether the friends she had visited since the funeral, had been quite so affable as in the past?

The public rebuke by her brother had been followed, immediately, by that of Mr. Collins. An occurrence so unlikely it had rendered her speechless and then, much later, thoughtful. It had forced on her the enormity of what she had proposed. His offer of a service at Rosings had been rapid and wise, but she had not been grateful, she had been resentful. He had been her dear affectionate puppy, she had never given him permission to bark. Two proper tears formed in Lady Catherine's eyes and rolled down her cheeks as she pondered on Mr. Collins. He had come to see her as a candidate for the restored Benefice, sponsored by Mr. Beevers at the prompting of the Countess. She could not, of course, refuse it to him, but she had been delighted with him from the beginning. Open faced, energetic and curious about everything, he had put her in mind of a lively clumsy puppy. His admiration for the house that she and her husband had built and loved was unfeigned. She had spent much time showing it to him, answering his questions, sharing with him the aggravations they had faced and conquered, and the extravagance necessary to achieve their ideal.

She had even summoned a small carriage and taken him *herself* to the Parsonage. They went round it together, each for the first time. His silent yearning had touched her as he moved in admiring absorption from room to room, and the expression of gratitude when she had told him that it was his had sealed a contract of deep mutual affection, further reinforced by their shocked hilarious laughter when they remembered the church, which they had both forgotten.

These pleasing recollections had brought some balm, the tears had ceased and did not resume as her thoughts moved to Fitzwilliam. He had asked her directly if she had accepted the dispatch intended for Mrs. Fountain, thus compelling her to lie. She could not excuse that. What she had done was right. There could be no relationship between her nephew and her Housekeeper, scandalous or otherwise. But, and here she admitted a fault, if one could be too quick in defending family honour, that was the fault. The greater fault, however, lay with the stupid soldier who had misled her, who had said that the letter was from Colonel Fitzwilliam, and must go urgently to Mrs. Fountain. She had been outraged. He deserved to be court martialed for misleading her and taking her nephew's name in vain. Now he wanted the thing back and it had disappeared. She had not touched it. It was too distasteful. She had left it on the table and swept it from her mind to go instantly to dismiss the woman who, smiling and respectful to the mistress, had treacherously seduced the visiting nephew. She shuddered at her part in that brief violent episode. Convinced of her guilt she had excised Mrs. Fountain from her memory, but now the woman came tumbling back, her shocked white face, first pleading then very angry, rising like a ghost. Why should Mrs. Fountain receive a military dispatch for which she had pledged her own signature? This new thought bewildered her further. She feared a court martial. Dreaded her signature being brought in evidence; dreaded that she might be personally involved. It would be a scandal. What would her brother say to her then? Nothing. He had not spoken to her since his rebuke. He would never speak to her again. Tears flowed again, gently and unnoticed, through half closed eyelids. Thus Alice found her and fetched Mrs. Jenkinson.

"Lady Catherine, we must send for the physician."

"I want Mr. Collins."

There he was, young and sturdy, not a puppy at all. His open face regarded her with affectionate concern. He fetched a chair and sat alongside her.

"I'm glad to see you at last. I was very concerned."

"Oh Mr. Collins!" She extended a hand as tears flowed again. He took the hand in a firm clasp.

"Lady Catherine, why are you so unhappy?" She told him. Lady Catherine under siege, capitulated to the young Parson, unloaded all her burdens, anxieties and misgivings upon him and having done so slipped gratefully into a sleep of exhaustion.

He returned thoughtfully to the Parsonage for dinner and confirmed to Charlotte that it was the same package that she had mentioned. Charlotte feared that Lady Catherine may have destroyed it but he was sure that she had not. She had said she could not bear to touch it and left it on the table. He did not know which table, but assumed the

PEGGY TULIP

messenger had been received in the small drawing room. The package had disappeared.

"Things do not disappear, Thomas. It has been moved."

They continued their meal in silence. Charlotte broke the silence.

"Dorcas could not read, and I was too embarrassed to ask Mrs.Wilby, but now find that she can. If someone who could read, saw the dispatch addressed to Mrs. Fountain in the small drawing room, would they not take it to her, or leave it for her in her room? And if it was left, and she had already been dismissed never to return, might it not still be where she would have been?"

He was staring in shock and admiration. He put down his knife and fork.

"I shall go and see Mrs. White."

Within half an hour he was running back elated, to tell her that she was absolutely right.

"Why did Mrs.White not find it?"

"She and her niece don't use that room. It has been unused since Mrs. Fountain went. There was a desk with a sloping lid, she lifted the lid and there was the dispatch."

"Oh Thomas! Can we send it to her?"

"The lieutenant has taken it and I have his signature." He waved a paper. "He is astounded, delighted and vindicated. He will be off as soon as they can saddle his horse."

He put his arms tightly round her, lifted her right off the ground, whirled her round then put her firmly back onto her feet. Perhaps he could dance after all!

"I seem to have married a Wise Woman."

CHAPTER

38

Charlotte visited Mrs. Allen with a letter for Mary Fountain, to let her know that the dispatch was now found, and how it had disappeared. Mrs. Allen greeted her in a state of suppressed excitement. She was impervious to receiving any news but bursting to transmit her own. She pressed on Charlotte an envelope of high quality, and spoke with awe.

"It contains one of these, my Dear." What she showed was an invitation to the wedding of Mary Anne Fountain and George Alfred Fitzwilliam, Baron Grendon of Calthorpe.

"Sit down, my Dear. You look quite startled, as I was myself. There is also a letter for you. These two invitations, yours and mine, have preceded all others by one week because they wanted us to be the first to know. Is it not wonderful?"

Charlotte gazed upon it, her emotions stirred.

"Oh, Mrs. Allen, may I embrace you?"

"I wish you would, my Dear." Embrace they did, tears of joy allowed to flow unhindered.

She returned home with a restlessness she could hardly contain. Thomas was pre-occupied and they shared their mid-day meal almost in silence, but she thought she saw the ghost of a smile. She told him of her visit, and that Mrs. Allen was in good spirits. He told her that he had given the receipt for the dispatch to Lady Catherine. They separated, he to his garden, she to her letter from Mary Fountain.

"My Very Dear, Very Good Friend, I wish to make known to you all that has happened." The writing was small, neat and close. Eager to know everything, she read carefully then laid it aside. Restlessness overwhelmed her. Had Thomas tried to conceal a smile? Could he have guessed their secret? She fetched a shawl and walked to the paddock. Both ponies grazed. When they were both grazing she knew Thomas was near, in church, study, garden or potting shed. She decided to remain until the ponies noticed her and came to nuzzle.

It must be the compounding dramas of Rosings that left her so teasingly unsettled, life was never like this at Lucas Lodge. She thought of the arrogance of Lady Catherine, stealing Mary Fountain's dispatch, and smiled at her retribution, a jolly good pummelling by the black cat! Suddenly, surrounded as she was by infinite air, she was gasping for breath and thought she might be about to discover what it was like to faint. The ponies had grazed towards her and were looking up. She grasped the paddock rail and leaned against it, forcing herself to breathe deeply and fought to re-gain self-possession. Feet pressed onto the earth, hands firmly on the paddock rail, good sense eased back into her. Breathing settled. She stood firmly up-right and admitted that the restlessness and uncertainties had nothing to do with the excitements and dramas of Rosings. They had generated within herself, Charlotte Lucas Collins, and sometimes life, itself, demanded the taking of un-calculable risks. These thoughts brought stillness, calm and strength. She was herself again. She smiled inwardly; she was more than herself. Having nothing better to give, she offered the backs of her hands for nuzzling then fondled the bony furry heads until the ponies shook themselves free.

She took her letter and a cushion to the potting shed where Thomas was doing some tidying up. He shook his head and gave her the pleased smile that she expected. As she re-read Mary Fountain's letter she glanced occasionally at him, seeing again the elusive half smile. She wondered whether a clergyman baptized his own children, whether the risk of meeting Lady Catherine would keep her mother from a Christening and how to persuade Thomas to talk to her about his father.

The strange events of her day were reflected in longer evening prayer, and she raised her head to find the blue eyes upon her.

"I suspect something unusual happened at Mrs. Allen's house this morning. Are you at liberty to tell me what?"

She passed him the unopened envelope and watched as he opened it and read the invitation. His face was a mask of surprise.

"We must keep it secret for a week. And what have you been secretly smiling about, are you at liberty to tell me?" He laughed out loud showing his teeth. The laughter was infectious. "Tell me Thomas!"

"Lady Catherine paid us a great compliment when I gave her the receipt and told her you had solved the mystery."

"She said something amusing?"

"That was not her intention."

"What did she say?"

"That we had made her very ...." He dissolved into laughter.

"Thomas! Very happy? Very grateful?" He was shaking his head, trying to say the word through laughter and eventually she thought she read it on his lips.

"Meek?" He nodded, laughter gone, tears wet on his cheeks. "Did you laugh?" He shook his head.

"But I've had several cheerful moments during the day."

Charlotte also shook her head, smiling broadly and wondering what word was the opposite of meek, for that word would perfectly describe Lady Catherine de Bourgh.

CHAPTER

39

Charlotte decided that the potting shed was a suitable place to ask Thomas whether a clergymen baptized his own children.

He seemed not to be surprised, but slightly uncertain. When might this be? Several months. Smiling and shaking his head he went back to his task then laughed out loud and told her she was an enigma. He was wearing the apron she had made for him and she was threading elastic into two half sleeves, from wrist to elbow, that would complete the task. She thought she observed, as she half watched him, a physical change, a bracing of the shoulders. It must be imagination.

"You would like me to tell you about my father." He had read her mind. "But first," he paused, "my mother. I was not yet three when she died and I have no recollectable memory of her, but I did suffer a cataclysmic loss, and it is you Charlotte who revealed to me what that loss was." His voice was unemotional, stating fact. "It was the loss of closeness and tenderness." She sat quite still. "No-one ever spoke to me of my mother, except Anne, and she came, surprisingly, into my life when I was just five years old and at my first boarding school. She remained in my life, spasmodically, for several months. I loved her visits. I loved her, but I cannot remember any detail of our conversations, except the warning about guarding the picture, when she gave it to me. It could only have been from her that I gained the conviction that my mother was an angel in heaven looking after me; and it was from her that I learned that her name was Isabella". Thomas had continued to work. Now he stopped, wiped his hands and leaned on the potting bench, smiling. "Is that not strange? I had never wondered. I didn't even know that I didn't know."

"I don't know how to describe *him*. An amiable looking man whose attitude to me was, I have come to think, disinterest tinged with malice. Not violent in any way at all but I was wary, moved away if he looked at me. It would never have occurred to me to ask him a question. He never mentioned my mother, no-one did, and I remember no trace of her in my home. You saw the place but it did not look like that in my childhood. It became increasingly ramshackle. I was hardly ever there for longer than a month or two at a time, always farmed out to various educational establishments. I really liked my schools, enjoyed the company, enjoyed the learning. I was never neglected or mistreated, but always expecting to be shifted elsewhere. I suspect he simply failed to pay. Money was his problem. When I was at home, the servants were amiable but transient. The place was lively, he entertained a lot of people. I heard, but I saw nothing of it, being too young.

When I was a tall lad of thirteen, however, I was deemed not to be too young. Welcomed and encouraged, I entertained his guests mightily on more than one occasion by drinking too much claret then sharing with them the fruits of my education. Within a month of that practice commencing, I was boarding with Mr. Beevers and never went back to my father except as an adult, by which time he was an invalid.

I always had that comforting sense that I was being watched-over by the Jesus part of God, interceded for by my mother who looked like an angel and lived secretly in a box. Thanks to the mysterious Anne, the Lord was my shepherd and my faith was absolute, whenever a chasm opened I expected God to shepherd me to the other side, and he did. Wiser at thirteen, my removal to Mr. Beevers made me suspect human intervention, so I asked him. He told me he could not lie but could not break a confidence.

I pressed my father on the matter when I visited him after graduation, to let him know that I intended taking Holy Orders. He was a very sick man. He offered me a bargain. He would answer any question I asked when the time came, in return for a good shriving and a good burial. He laughed as he spoke then cursed, as his laughter turned to coughing. This was not a man I could love, though I could not be indifferent to him. I certainly could not shrive or bury him. I delayed my ordination until after he died. His funeral was well attended. I was with a number of strangers at the back of the church, several of whom had a lien on my home. I found it impossible to pray for him and still do." He looked up and gave her a wry smile. "That last visit was when I was made aware of the entail on Longbourn. How only the death of the inconsiderate Bennet would relieve his problems. I was astonished that I actually had some relations, including five female cousins; a complete whole family with parents! Treasure indeed. He pulled a wry face. It is fanciful but I thought I detected something of my father in Mr. Bennett, a general attitude of casual disinterest."

They lapsed into silence as he bent again to his plants and Charlotte dwelt for a moment on an hysterical Mrs. Bennet and her daughters being flung without mercy out of Longbourn.

"Did you think it was Lady Catherine?"

"Watching over? Yes, for a time. It seemed obvious. Mr. Beevers had sent me to her, I was newly ordained and it was a benefice far beyond my reach, but he said nothing. When I came to Hunsford I expected Lady Catherine to tell me, but she said nothing, and she is not a woman to be reticent about that kind of generosity." Charlotte smiled to herself at this mild admission of Lady Catherine's imperfection.

"You never asked him again?"

"Would you?"

"No. It's all very strange."

"Strange indeed, imagine having to tell all that to Lady Lucas. It gives me nightmares to think of it."

Charlotte smiled. The letter was already composing itself in her head.

40

Waiting for Thomas to return from Rosings, Charlotte carefully un-picked a dozen silken stitches. It took twice as long as it had taken her to put them in; the scar in the linen was a reproach. Mrs. Jenkinson, at a loss, had sent again for Thomas to minister to Lady Catherine and Charlotte had allowed her concentration to wander from the precision of each stitch to a disturbing empathy with Lady Catherine in her new difficulty. She had known that an invitation to Mary Fountain's wedding would loose the black cat upon her again, which was, of course, exactly what she deserved but ... one could feel compassion.

Her Ladyship had recovered rapidly after the departure of the Lieutenant with the dispatch from Mrs. Fountain's desk. She had invited the Parson and his wife to dine, unexpectedly, the next day and she had been especially charming and good natured with Charlotte. The good nature had continued over their next normal dining day.

Charlotte had been on tenterhooks since receiving their own invitation to the wedding, not knowing whether there would be any wedding invitations for Rosings. Yesterday there had been three and they had caused complete astonishment. Miss de Bourgh and Mrs. Jenkinson had been excited and delighted and pleased that the Collins were also invited. The intriguing mystery of the situation had overwhelmed anything else of interest at that dinner, which they had taken with Miss de Bourgh, because Lady Catherine had relapsed.

Her invitation to the wedding, a bolt of lightning from a clear sky, had stunned Lady Catherine. Disbelieving, she had pushed it into a drawer and spent the day in her own rooms in a state of irritation. When she rose in the morning, after an appallingly restless night, she was convinced that she had dreamed that it was a nightmare and rushed to the guilty drawer to discover that it was not. The whole thing was impossible, she could not believe it true. Holding the dreadful thing between thumb and forefinger, she read it carefully for the first time. Replies were to go to the Countess. This detail cast her into outer realms of doubt and despair and sent her reeling back to the refuge of the chaise longue. She closed her eyes and lay back with a deep hopeless sigh. She recalled the exquisite deep satisfaction of her revenge on the housekeeper but remembered the rising wrath on which she had turned her back. Fitzwilliam, least considered of her nephews, to whom she had lied without hesitation when he asked about the missing dispatch, would be next Head of the Family. She had escaped the humiliation of a court martial to fall into the excruciating private degradation of being slighted for life by her housekeeper, the next Lady Grendon, who would be the next Countess of Raimond. She faced a lifetime of small mortifications, perhaps a lonely exile from the family and from their homes, and a prolonged wilting in her most desired and treasured friendships.

Lady Catherine had never experienced self-doubt in her adult life until these last weeks when it had fallen on her in crushing waves. Tears seeped once more from under closed eyelids. Alice, her maid, finding her again in a deep listless state of misery, had resorted to Mrs. Jenkinson who had resorted in turn to Mr. Collins.

"Lady Catherine?" She opened her eyes to see his young face, serious with concern for her and extended a despairing hand, which he took. She closed her eyes again and unburdened onto him her deepest miseries; what she had done to Mrs. Fountain and how that lady now had both the power and the reason to exact a terrible revenge. He squeezed the hand sympathetically and spoke softly.

"You were over hasty Lady Catherine. It was an act of theft." She opened her eyes, startled. He nodded. "By taking that official dispatch, you deprived her of access to her capital and cut off all access to her income." He paused. "And by dismissing her you rendered her homeless. The innocent homeless pauper had good reason to wonder at your malice."

She had raised herself stiffly on the chaise longue staring at him in shock, then collapsed helplessly backwards with a whimper. Further tears from a not quite exhausted store seeped from under the eyelids and her body moved with a last attempt at sobs. He softly rubbed the hand and waited until she was still and silent. When he spoke again his voice was different, stimulating.

"But there is something very odd here, do you not think so?" He paused in thought. "She sent you an invitation to her wedding." He paused again. "A vengeful woman would take pleasure in not sending you an invitation, would cut you out of her life." He nodded at the eyes now fixed on his, pausing, considering. "If you regret what you did, you would tell her so, ask her to forgive you." The listless hand stiffened slightly. "You would ask her whether she wishes you to attend, or stay away from her wedding, and respect her decision."

He watched as the eyes opened wider and the lips tightened. The hand was sharply withdrawn. He retrieved it and held it, against her resistance, in a firm two-handed grip. He smiled into her outraged face. He spoke slowly.

"She has charitably offered you an escape route from the future you dread. Take it. Do not let a wrong fester. Write the letter, give it to me, and I will see that she gets it." He gave her a look that was undoubtedly tender; resisted the temptation to touch her tortured face. "You are exhausted, Lady Catherine. Close your eyes and have a sleep."

He gave the hand a parting squeeze and returned it gently. Lady Catherine, like a bewildered wizened child, closed her eyes and slept.

He returned, with relief, to the calm of the Parsonage. When Charlotte raised a questioning eyebrow he shook his head and smiled.

"Goodness knows! I hardly dare to hope."

When Alice came later to inquire if Lady Catherine would go to dinner, she found her seated at her desk with one letter for Mr. Collins, one for delivery to the Earl at Gavelston and five more for delivery to friends. She was very quiet but insisted that her efforts had not exhausted her and that she required to dress. She was amenable, invited Alice to choose suitable garments and accepted everything. She sat uncomplaining and unmoving as her hair was teased and offered up her face with closed eyes. Alice saw her off to dinner, tidied the room thoughtfully, then went to share her opinion with the household that Lady Catherine was very seriously ill.

The letter to Mrs. Fountain had been very difficult to start, but surprisingly easy to accomplish. She had done exactly what Mr. Collins had suggested, and the act of signing the letter had suddenly released an unexpected flood of relief. She had sought and found similar relief in signing the others, and luxuriated in her meekness.

Miss De Bourgh had arranged dinner and Lady Catherine was welcomed, with appropriate formality, as a guest of her daughter, to dine in her own breakfast room. In her altered state and unaccustomed surroundings she remembered, with a pang, that this charming handsome young woman was her only child and the older one, her oldest friend, and greeted each appropriately and affectionately.

After dinner the old friends fell into the highs and lows of long gone days and Anne listened as the two women who had reared and trained her, revealed their truthful younger characters in reminiscence. She knew now, for certain, that the greatest gift her mother had given her was the friendship of Mrs. Jenkinson. She heard of Lady Catherine's remorse at the rift from her sister Anne, and of spiteful acts caused by jealousy of a friendship. Deep sadness overwhelmed them for a time as Mrs. Jenkinson, daughter of a scholar, wife of a scholar, revealed to them the tragic loss of a clever daughter, an only child eleven years old, whom doctors had leeched to death. When Lady Catherine came seeking a governess for her little girl she had had little hesitation in leaving a once happy home, now saddened by two tragedies, and removing herself to Rosings. The tender eyes of mother and tutor had rested on Anne, who had eluded the leeches, and all had embraced affectionately before retiring.

CHAPTER

41

Two days before the wedding Thomas handed Charlotte a letter, elegant as to hand and paper. Formally addressed and written on behalf of the Countess of Raimond, it invited him to be present two hours before the wedding at her London home for a discussion. Her Ladyship hoped that his wife would consent to accompany him.

Punctual, they presented themselves at the London mansion. In a drawing room on the first floor were Mr. Beevers, Mr. Darcy and a tall handsome woman dressed in black. Quick and beaming with pleasure she introduced herself, took Charlotte by the elbow and led her to a chair, one of five, around a small table. The others followed.

"I am so glad to meet you Mrs. Collins, I have learned such good things of you. And you also Mr. Collins, though in private and with your permission, I shall call you Tom. I know that you are all previously acquainted. Let us sit down."

Thomas stopped moving, his voice was uncertain.

"Why do you call me Tom?"

She smiled at him and touched his arm gently.

"Because I am your friend, and before that, I was the friend of your friend Anne who always referred to you as Tom."

"But who *was* Anne? *Why* was she my friend?"

The Countess and Mr. Beevers stared at him open mouthed, then at each other. She recovered first.

"Anne was Isabella's friend when they were at school in Scarborough."

"She was my mother, Mr. Collins." Said Mr. Darcy. "You and I, it seems, are old acquaintance." He extended a hand, which the dazed Thomas took. "I am glad to be reacquainted."

"Anne was your mother? You were the boy?"

"I was the boy."

Thomas turned towards the Countess.

"You know about me?"

"Forgive me. I know all about you. I inherited you from Anne." She shook her head, in apology. "Clearly I have been remiss."

"No! You have been my guardian angel! I trusted you and you never betrayed my trust." He looked round for Charlotte who was wide eyed and open mouthed.

"Charlotte you heard all this? Can you believe it?"

Her voice was uncertain.

"Thomas, I see no reason to disbelieve it."

"Then I must try hard to believe it myself."

He looked at the smiling Countess, at the smiling Mr. Darcy and the smiling Mr. Beevers, tutor, guardian and what else...conduit … go between?

"Mr. Beevers, I think we have never shaken hands." Mr. Beevers extended his hand.

Thomas looked at the still bewildered face of Charlotte, shook himself and huffed a great breath that expressed pleasure, surprise, disbelief and everything he could not find words for. Everyone laughed with relief.

The Countess indicated the empty chairs and they sat.

"Tom, my nephew brought some trinkets from his home in Derbyshire. They will interest you. Darcy!"

Mr. Darcy smiled at Charlotte with a pleasing eagerness. He had before him three dark green leather cases, which he opened to display three silver-framed likenesses of young girls, and laid them before Mr. and Mrs. Collins.

"Anne!" said Thomas. "Charlotte, this is Anne."

"And here is your mother," said Charlotte. "And"… Discerning a resemblance in the third, "Could that be Lady Catherine?"

"Well done Mrs. Collins!" Mr. Darcy explained. "The likeness I saw on your wall, I knew I had seen it at Pemberley, but could not recall in what connection. It was easily found and when I saw the three together I remembered the story. The girls met at school in Scarborough. Isabella and Anne became the firmest of friends. Isabella was a regular visitor to Gavelston and a favourite of my grandfather who commissioned the pictures for himself and gave them later to my mother. The artist whom *she* commissioned to make the copy for you is, alas, no longer with us but I think you will agree I have found his equal." He laid two copies before them. "Compare them. I think you should have a likeness of your childhood friend, Anne, and of Lady Catherine also. They are my gift to you and Mrs. Collins."

Neither Charlotte nor her husband had the words to thank him. What he read in their faces was sufficient for Mr. Darcy.

"Tom," said the Countess, "some years ago you asked Mr. Beevers a direct question and he gave you an equivocal answer."

"He could not lie but he could not breach a confidence."

She nodded smiling, "We can speak of this, the four of us," she indicated the smiling Mr. Beevers and Charlotte, "at some time in the very near future." She looked at Mr. Darcy.

"My mother kept a Journal all her life," said Mr. Darcy. "I cannot let it leave Pemberley but will ask the Librarian to seek out those volumes that refer to Isabella and to yourself and would welcome you to study, perhaps even copy it. My Aunt and Mr. Beevers are even now deciding the dates of a future visit. You are most welcome to join them."

Once again Charlotte and Thomas were struck dumb.

"I so look forward to that," said the Countess. "There is much explaining to be done, but for now, my dear Tom, I will simply tell you that for all your life as a child you were under the watchful, benevolent eye of a clergyman such as yourself, indeed several of them since you moved more often than any clergyman is likely to do. Also I wanted you to learn from me that I bought your childhood home. Its next occupants will be my son and daughter-in-law. I hope that will not distress you and think we can assume that it will be a home where you and Mrs. Collins will always be received with a welcome."

Charlotte stared on Thomas's dazed face, willing him to ask the question that was on her own mind.

"Mrs. Collins?" The Countess was smiling at her.

Charlotte took hold of Thomas's hand.

"May I ask, who was Isabella Aston?"

Thomas's hand tightened on hers.

"I can answer that," said the Countess. "Isabella Aston of Dore, in the County of Derbyshire, was an orphan and a considerable heiress whose fortune, during her minority was squandered by those who should have guarded it. She married, much beneath herself, for love, and died bearing her second child, a daughter who also died. I only learned these things from Anne, who became my sister-in-law and friend."

As Thomas's hand had tightened and loosened on her own, Charlotte welcomed the timely distraction of two footmen entering the room to prepare a table.

"A little refreshment," announced the Countess. "Then, change for the wedding!"

Charlotte and Mrs. Allen had spoken of the coming event at every opportunity. They had wondered if Lady Catherine would be present, or Mrs. Fountain's sister and the dreaded brother-in-law. Mrs. Allen, experienced in military weddings had prepared Charlotte for the splendour of the dress uniforms and warned her not to be startled at the clash of half-drawn sabres from the guard of honour at the mention of 'impediment'

Alas, the colonel was the only soldier present and he was not in uniform. Mrs. Allen, to whom the colonel was an absolute hero, thought he might have refrained, so as not to put Mr. Darcy in the shade. She did concede however, watching the two men in conversation with Mr. Beevers at the altar, that she would happily have walked up the aisle to marry either of them. The small church was filled with arrangements of flowers and a string orchestra played in a gallery.

Charlotte and Thomas had arrived with Mrs. Allen, Lottie and Dorcas in the coach of Mrs. Allen's obliging son but in the church they were separated. Thomas and Charlotte were led, as guests of the bridegroom, to sit behind Lady Catherine, Miss de Bourgh and Mrs. Jenkinson. As they parted Mrs. Allen gave Charlotte a pat on the arm and a brief smile that said no-one could have been a better friend of the bride than Mrs. Collins, then she followed a sides-man to join Sir William and Lady Lucas across the aisle. Charlotte and her mother, across the gap that separated them, exchanged smiles that shared the secret that each was dressed as they had been for Charlotte's own wedding.

Facing forward, admiring the flowers and the altar dressings, Charlotte resisted the temptation to peer round in an attempt to find and identify Mrs. Fountain's sister. Surrendering herself to the music she pondered the collision and collusion of friendships that had touched Thomas. Friendship she decided was a second cousin to Love, a wholesome mysterious thing of varying intensities and, of course, a wilful crosser of social boundaries. She undoubtedly felt friendship for Mrs. Wilby and thought it reciprocated, and what of her mother and Molly, and the Countess and Mr. Beevers? She started, excitedly, in her seat. Thomas came out of his own deep thoughts and turned towards her placing a hand on her knee in concern. She patted his hand then settled back to smile at the flowers around the altar. Thomas and Lady Catherine! Friendship, of course! Wholesome, mysterious and wilful!

At a signal, the bridegroom and best man rose, bowed into the church to welcome the Earl and Countess in splendour. They had left off their mourning for the wedding of the heir, and acknowledging guests on either side, took seats behind the bridegroom. They were accompanied by a Bishop and by a military Dress Uniform splendid enough to convince Charlotte that Mrs. Allen had not exaggerated, but she could not think that this proud mature gentleman would rattle his sabre.

Immediately, there was music again and a stir from the rear. Charlotte did turn her head but her eyes filled with tears as Mary Fountain and her companions moved to stand before the altar and inexplicably they did so again as the newly joined couple walked away from the altar. Charlotte was obliged to rely on the memory of Mrs. Allen to learn how her friend was dressed for her wedding, for when she appeared later at a Wedding Breakfast, she had changed for the journey to her new home.

The smallness of the party at the reception compelled intimacy. Charlotte learned from the Dress Uniform that he was not the Colonel's commanding officer as she had supposed, but his godfather. She observed her mother and Lady Catherine conversing in good humour as her father nodded his head. It made her smile. Her parents, having wagered against the obvious favourite, were delighted to be the winners. To their great surprise and gratification the prize had been the enviable social dividend of close friendship with Lord and Lady Grendon; they could afford to be gracious with the loser.

Mrs. Fountain's relations seemed a stylish, handsome couple. Custom and practice had prevailed and he, the only male within her family, had given her in marriage, an irony relished by Charlotte and Mrs. Allen, while she, the sister, had stood Matron of Honour. Affection between the sisters had been evident and any old resentments of the brother-in-law if they still existed, seemed neutralized by the prestigious marriage.

Lady Catherine, very grand in old gold and carefully touched up by the artistic Alice, was rather eclipsed by her daughter, not so grand but gracefully tall and elegant in swathed pink, her quick smiles and new liveliness giving the lie to any rumour that she was an invalid. The Earl, who seemed to have forgotten that Catherine even had a daughter, was very taken with her and discovering from the Countess who she was, advanced on his sister berating her light heartedly for concealing this bright family light under a bushel. Charlotte, observing how Lady Catherine shrank from his approach and diminished further under the mild reprimand, felt some sympathy for her and looked covertly at the lined face of this proud and powerful man. He took his sister's hand.

"To reply to your letter would have given me too much pain but I do thank you for it. And I admire that you have atoned for a lifetime's hatred of the mother with a valuable benefice for her son."

This sentence surprised Lady Catherine as much as it surprised Charlotte, and as she was looking round for Thomas, Lady Catherine was doing the same. He was talking to the newly wedded couple who were preparing to depart for their new home. They, attracted by the simultaneous notice of a double gaze, moved towards them and made their farewells. Mrs. Collins and Lady Grendon held hands and looked into each other's eyes in an exchange that was beyond words. Once again Charlotte sensed a shrinking in Lady Catherine and then relief at the ease with which she was addressed, and her hand taken, by her new relation, but she noticed that Lady Catherine's hand was not taken by Lord Grendon, as was her own and those of her parents. 'Vulnerable' and 'Lady Catherine' were not words that sat easily alongside. She marvelled that two malicious acts of Lady Catherine against Mary Fountain should have rebounded so spectacularly against herself as to rearrange the landscape of their future lives in Mary Fountain's favour. Serendipity! Happy Happenstance!

She looked carefully for moment at a serene Mary Fountain as she leaned in kindness towards a shrinking, uncertain, Lady Catherine. These two had become an Allegory. An Allegory of Hubris overcome by Serendipity! Charlotte smiled at her own brilliant perception then realized that she was smiling at Lady Catherine who was smiling, rather uncertainly, back at her. A pricking conscience told her that she had given Lady Catherine little opportunity to return a genuine smile so she renewed it and added a friendly nod, which her husband's friend reciprocated and then turned towards Thomas.

"Mr. Collins!" Thomas turning at the call gave Lady Catherine the opportunity to recognize the blue eyes of Isabella Aston. "The carriage is returning to Rosings, Mr. Collins if we can be of service."

"You are very kind Lady Catherine but we travelled here with Mrs. Allen. We go now to thank the Countess and say our farewells." He took Charlotte's hand and as they went she wondered if making those farewells would be yet another ordeal for Lady Catherine.

Alongside Mrs. Allen was Dorcas with Lottie, asleep on her shoulder. They said their farewells for these two were not returning with Mrs. Allen but were bound, astonishingly, for Thomas's old home. Dorcas, who seemed to believe that she owed her good fortune to Charlotte, always beamed upon her and Charlotte was relieved that she bore no ill will. She looked at the sleeping child for whom she had developed a deep affection and remembered, indeed would never forget, how the future of each of them had simultaneously balanced precariously on a moment in time, for good fortune or ill. She thought of Lottie's father, whose imagined fury had stoked the fires of her own anger into the desperate reckless act that had brought them to this conclusion. It could have been otherwise. She took Thomas's hand gratefully and climbed, with her dear friend Mrs. Allen, into the coach that would take them home.

Divested of finery and ready to retire, they were at their prie-dieux. Charlotte, saturated in gratitude, knelt open-eyed letting it flow word-lessly Heavenward. She watched Thomas's bowed head. Not the Third Collect tonight, tonight was different. Thomas was different. The rev-elations of Mr. Darcy and the Countess had touched him like a magic wand and the mysterious promise of Anne's journal was a Holy Grail.

When they walked away from their first meeting with the Countess he had been Thomas, of course, but an enhanced Thomas. Crucial miss-ing pieces had been fitted into the patchwork of his life and more were promised. He was reflective, twice blessed. Others would not have no-ticed it in the course of the long eventful day but his good-humoured con-fidence and quiet self-assurance had filled Charlotte with tender pride. She was grateful that she had met him before he was enhanced, while he was still naive enough to get himself into such a pickle that he would clutch the sleeve of a near-stranger and drag her into the shrubbery. She closed her eyes and thanked God for that, when she opened them his blue eyes were upon her.

"Something happened today that was strange and wonderful."

She laughed out loud. The day had been packed full with strange and wonderful things! She asked where it had it happened.

"In the Chapel, before the wedding, listening to the music I found myself thinking of my father and praying for him." She was startled. This *was* strange and wonderful. Thomas nodded. "He could have been a man unused to tenderness who found it, responded, gave himself wholly up to it and lost it. What desolation! Perhaps all I witnessed was his desolation."

She was not entirely won over.

"He could have been kinder to his child." She paused, and made her own surprising confession. "I prayed for Lady Catherine. I had to. I sat behind her and watched her fidget with nerves. I am become too sensitive to her feelings. I must see less of her."

It was Thomas's turn to laugh aloud.

"Perhaps you should see more of her." He studied her. "Why do you resist Rosings?"

She told him, relating with ease and some amusement the trials of her first two visits to Rosings while he watched her in growing wonder.

"I felt I had disgraced you and my mother. I could not speak of it to either of you. My relief lay in Mary Fountain and my mother said she could not be my friend because she was a servant."

"It seems to me that your natural friend is Mrs. Jenkinson. She has become a Classical scholar Charlotte, I defer to her. She wants to study Chapman's Homer with Anne and was wondering if you might like to join them."

Charlotte was thrilled.

"Really?

"Yes, that would take you willingly to Rosings."

"Thomas!" She was staring at him. Laughing.

"Yes?"

"If Lady Catherine was at school with your mother, so was Mrs. Jenkinson! We must have her to tea, with Anne. Tell them the revelations we have had.

The excitements of the day had stimulated rather than tired them. They took chairs before the embers and ash in the fireplace. He definitely wanted Charlotte to be with him when he showed their new pictures to

Lady Catherine. She warned him of the Earl's remark that had startled both herself and Lady Catherine.

"Hated my mother! Goodness! We shall have to discover why. You've got to be there." He paused, "I will help you to face your dragon if you will help me to face mine."

Who could his dragon possibly be she wondered?

"I have two. Your mother and Mrs. Bennet."

They laughed together and she thought it extraordinary that Lady Catherine had never been a dragon to Thomas.

She assured him that when her mother received an account of this morning's revelations she would become a Fairy Godmother. Unfortunately, she could give no such assurance about Mrs. Bennet. If that lady resented the loss of the old Thomas as a son in law, the loss of the enhanced Thomas would be a bitter draught indeed. His escape had been miraculous. Uneasy in his conscience about the entail, he had gone to offer himself as husband for one, *any* one it seemed, of the five potentially dispossessed daughters of Mr. and Mrs. Bennet. He had gone to Longbourn, complacent perhaps, but in the hope of finding, and becoming, part of a real family by marrying into it. Charlotte had witnessed his desperate humiliating rejection, an encounter that must have left its scars. Her love had rescued him and won her the implacable enmity of Mrs. Bennet. She thought it unlikely that they would associate much in future. Even the enhanced Thomas would not go to Longbourn willingly, but the Bennets could not be shunned when she and Thomas visited Meryton. She cherished her friendship with Lizzie and the parents were old friends.

"None of us can choose our relatives Thomas. You will just have to get used to Mrs. Bennet and she will have to get used to you. However," she offered her advice slowly and seriously, "when she is overwhelming you, lapse into deep silence and perfect stillness, and in that quiet state, slowly reflect and consider what your feelings would be if she was your mother-in-law." Then it came, almost perfected, the expression she had cherished and nourished, bemusement; on the edge of laughter, at a loss for words, the slow shaking of the head and the blue eyes filled with humour.

He stood. She moved towards him and rested her cheek against his buttons, night buttons, flat and covered with linen, so much more comfortable than the day buttons, and the large comforting arms came round behind.

THE END

PEGGY TULIP

About the Author

On her eighty fifth birthday Peggy Tulip, was at a loose end and seeking an occupation. She decided to attempt a rescue of the unfortunate Charlotte Lucas who had been so uncharitably parked by Jane Austen in the Parsonage at Huntan, with the intolerably insensitive and self-absorbed Reverend Collins. From her earliest readings of Pride and Prejudice this cruel coupling had roused unease. Not much chance of real happiness there. Charlotte Lucas deserved better. Perhaps a little probing insight into both characters might reveal a more promising future? Once you start you never know where you'll end up! Hopefully with a quiet launch of a quiet little book that might find a way into the world.